LOST
OBLIVION

LOST OBLIVION

A WILD OBLIVION NOVELLA

BY

KATHERINE SILVA

Strange Wilds Press

Published by Strange Wilds Press
Kindle first edition: October 12th, 2023
Print first edition: October 12th, 2023

Cover design by Katherine Silva
www.katherinesilvaauthor.com
Strange Wilds Press Logo by MartaLeo
Cover photos courtesy of Pexels and Unsplash

THE HOWLING OWL BAR

9 P.M.
SATURDAY NIGHT

The noise behind the door foretold the liveliness of the Howling Owl Bar. The evening was just getting started. Hank stood outside on the sidewalk and tried to force the memories from his phone conversation with Melissa back into the foggy depths of his mind.

The shouting. The names she'd called him. The things he'd said in return.

He wasn't sure if she'd taken something before she called him. Her unhinged rage hinted to him that she had. And that it all seemed to come out of nowhere. She had promised she was going to get clean; she was going to do better for Evie. His suspicions pushed him to a tipping point.

"Do you even love her?" Hank had finally shouted to cut Melissa's tirade short. "Do you even care about your own daughter anymore? Do you know what it does to her every time she sees you like this?"

Melissa had hung up.

He'd already planned on going out that night. Thank God, Melissa had called when he was driving to the bar and not in the living room where Evie would have heard it all. Even if Hank had tried to spare her and take it into the bedroom, there was only so much privacy he could find in their tiny apartment. Evie would still have heard and she'd have figured out what the call was about. Though she was only six, Evie had experienced enough of their disagreements and fights to put two and two together.

Right now, Hank wanted nothing more than to shed the misery of that phone call; to drink a few beers and to play some pool with his friend, Gerard, to help fade the fight into the background. He pulled open the door and let the vibe from The Howling Owl pour over him.

Booths lined the right side of the bar, filled with patrons laughing and sipping their brews and cocktails. Hank nodded to Bob and Keri, the owners of the plant nursery. Keri chirped a quick "hi" before blocking a straw-wrapper dart being blown at her by their daughter. Bob corralled their youngest son, Jason, back into the booth as he tried to duck under the table for an escape. Jason and Evie were in the same grade and played together at the park every other weekend.

Dan Cooper, Hank's boss, was warming up at the karaoke mic with his cover of an Eagle's song. Hank knew it well; one of his favorite songs. The crowd, men and women Hank recognized from about town, cheered enthusiastically at Dan's timbre.

Andy Marušić, a member of Pemigewasset Valley's

Search and Rescue who worked closely with the park rangers and was Dan's biggest rival at karaoke night, gave him a loud clap for encouragement and giggled at something one of the others said nearby. He locked eyes with Hank and waved. "You never texted me back. What are you: ghosting me?" he called.

Hank returned the wave and put a finger to his ear to gesture he couldn't hear Andy, even if he could. Andy had texted him about joining himself and Dan for his birthday celebration in a few weeks. While Hank would have enjoyed a weekend fishing trip with the two, it was unlikely he and Dan would be able to take time off the same weekend and Hank wasn't sure he wanted to ask. He'd spent a number of days off as it were with Melissa and her need to be at rehab. Needing to take care of Evie.

He continued searching the crowd for Gerard. Usually, Gerard could be found amongst the others, laughing dryly and drinking an IPA. The choice of beer, Hank learned, was as a tribute to the memory of his son, David.

That night, Hank located his friend's gawky form hunched over a stool at the bar, scrolling through some text on his phone. *No doubt reading some scientific paper on mushroom growth or moss*, Hank thought as he edged through the milling crowds of people to reach the bar. Gerard participated in a study for the University of New England on bryology and used to be a field researcher in his youth.

Hank touched Gerard on the shoulder as he started to pull a stool out from the counter.

Gerard jerked before his eyes caught on Hank's

appearance and an uneasy smile overtook his features.

"Easy there, Gerry," Hank said, sitting down next to him.

"Sorry, Hank. I haven't been getting much sleep," the older man said dismissively. "What are you in the mood for? Looks like Ford's got some Allagash White on tap."

"That sounds perfect."

The two of them settled in, getting through the pleasantries of how each other's days were. How was Gerard's wife, Penny? How was Evie? How was that violin concert that Gerard went to see in Boston on Thursday? How was Evie's class play? Did she enjoy her part as a bumblebee?

Eventually, the seven-minute silent mark bled in. They drank their beer and listened to Andy sing his rendition of Paul Simon's "You Can Call Me Al", though he had tweaked the lyrics to be "You Can OK My Corral". It was a classic move by Andy to try and one-up Dan's performances with his own parodies of popular songs.

Hank thought about how Gerard jumped when he'd touched him. His friend had been edgy ever since what had happened to them two weeks ago: an incident that was still aflutter on everyone's lips around town.

The missing teens. Shimmering Rock. The no doubt rabid bear that had killed three of them and left the fourth traumatized in the hospital. The creature had nearly killed Hank had Gerard not been there to save him from falling to his death...

Hank had dreamed about it off and on, waking with night sweats, unsure where he was. He woke poor Evie each time and she called out to him in terror, thinking something was happening to him each time. He hated waking her, worrying her. But that thing he'd encountered haunted him, its shining eyes like moonlight, what he'd seen it do to those poor kids…

Hank cleared his throat. "I called up to Cardend Memorial where they took that girl who survived the night up on the ridge…"

"Gina," Gerard said, his tone guarded.

"The nurses say she still hasn't come out of it. Been in a vegetative state for the last week or so. Before that, she was jumping at shadows. Any time anyone touched her…"

"Having a bear horrifically kill all of her friends in front of her would do that, I suppose." Gerard sipped at his beer.

"Do you ever dream about what happened?" Hank asked so suddenly it took him by surprise. "Do you ever wonder about what we saw up there on Shimmering Rock?"

Gerard glanced up from his glass but didn't make eye contact with Hank. "Yeah."

"I don't think it was a bear," Hank said. "I didn't see much. But… I can't stop seeing what happened to that kid right in front of me. It was—"

"Hank," Gerard interrupted, his voice stern. "Let's not. We're here. We're alive. We should enjoy the night, listen to Dan and Andy, drink our beer… We have to live in the here and now, don't we? We have to stay in the present."

There was an insistence behind Gerard's tone that made Hank's voice die off. Hank had been the only one to see that thing up there…whatever it was. He had also suffered a concussion. The headaches these last couple of weeks had been just as frequent as the nightmares. Maybe it had all been in his head after all? Maybe the things he thought he remembered never actually happened?

The song on the speakers changed to "Carry On My Wayward Son" by Kansas and Dan and Andy chimed in together, their grins broad. The crowd that had gathered around the bar hooped and hollered. Hank spotted Alicia, Dan's wife, in the crowd as she let out a sharp whistle in support.

Gerard's attention was back on the karaoke bar. He clapped enthusiastically and took another long pull from his beer. The mood of their conversation seemed all but forgotten.

Hank buried his lingering bewilderment, let the questions about what had happened sink back down into the muddled parts of his brain. He finished his beer and signaled to Ford, the bartender and owner, for another one. He let his own mouth curl into a grin as he watched his two co-workers belt out the upbeat tune, both leaning in close to the one mic.

He was alive. He was with his friends. Hank wanted to focus on the good.

He wished he had known then it would be the last time he would see Gerard face-to-face.

HANK'S APARTMENT

10 A.M.
SUNDAY MORNING

"What'll it be, Eves?" Hank glanced over his shoulder toward her at the kitchen table. "Waffles or pancakes today?"

"Pancakes!" Evie cheered.

In spite of the gray day outside, his daughter's smile brightened up the room and a warm happiness swelled in his chest at the sight of it. Sundays were their days together. He wouldn't need to return to the ranger station until that evening. He wasn't looking forward to it in light of last night's talk with Melissa. She'd pushed back Evie's drop-off time at her house, which meant he'd be likely getting to his shift late again.

Granted, Dan and everyone else at the ranger station had been understanding when Hank had found out about Melissa's addiction, with Hank being there for her and needing to take more time off to care for Evie. But it had been close to six months now, one month since he and

Melissa had officially separated, and Melissa's constant changing of pick-ups and drop-offs meant he wasn't reliable at his job. It showed he couldn't be depended on and that put his career in jeopardy.

Not only that, it was impossible to create consistency for Evie. She needed stability. She needed a schedule that didn't change every week.

As Hank heaped the pancake mix into a glass bowl with his measuring cup, he fantasized about how the drop-off would go that night. Whether or not Melissa would meet them at the driveway or stand on the doorstep as she'd been apt to do the last week. Would they exchange words at all? Worse yet, was she going to say something to Evie about how "inflexible" he was to accommodate her needs?

She'd done this once before. And when Evie had burst out in tears that he wasn't making enough time for Mommy's needs on their way back home, Hank had grown cold and sad and sick. He had explained to Evie that he and Melissa had to spend time apart, that they had both changed and realized they wanted and needed different things: things they couldn't give each other anymore. But that those changes would never affect how much they loved Evie.

Trying to explain to a six-year-old the complexities of Daddy's and Mommy's broken relationship was hard. It had only grown harder. He wanted nothing more than to spare her from all of the toxicity the addiction had caused in their family. He wanted her to understand that he had had to make a choice for her safety and for both of their well-beings.

"Daddy?"

He looked up. "Yes?"

"Can we go to the playground today?"

Splinters of rain struck the windows that looked out on the river behind their house. The sky revealed black thunderheads closing in. In the distance, the low rumble made the hairs on his arms raise slightly.

He cracked two eggs into the bowl. "Not today, hun. The slide will be wet. The sandbox will be messy. Angel can take you Monday after you get home from school, okay?"

Angel was Evie's after-school sitter, one of the few responsible teens with a driver's license who didn't have a job in retail over in North Conway or didn't participate in after-school sports.

Evie huffed. "Stupid rain."

"Hey," Hank said softly. "Rain is great! We can still go for a walk downtown. Jump in some of the puddles? Get some hot chocolate at Anne's after we stop at the hardware store?"

"Yes!" she proclaimed. After a moment, "Daddy, can you make hot chocolate pancakes?"

Hank smirked. "Not this morning. But if we have hot chocolate with breakfast, you won't be able to enjoy it later."

Evie's brow puckered at the statement. "But I love hot chocolate. Why wouldn't I enjoy it later?"

"Well, it's a treat. And if you have treats all the time, they kind of stop being special, don't they?"

"I suppose," she said with a sigh.

He chuckled. She'd learned the word "suppose" from one of her new favorite books at the library, *Suppose Your Nose*, and had been peppering her language with it over the last couple of days.

Hank finished mixing the batter together and flipped on the burner to heat up the stove top. Evie clambered over and climbed up on her pale blue stool to help throw a pad of butter into the pan. After a few seconds, it sizzled. Hank rolled his wrist to move the pan around and coat it.

Then, with him helping, Evie spooned in a ladelful of batter and they watched it cook, bubbles emerging around the edges of the circle.

The normalcy of the morning seeped into him, made him feel a tranquility that he'd struggled with ever since the horror he'd experienced in the mountains a couple weeks back. He drank his coffee, held it in his mouth for a few moments before swallowing, and watched Evie's fascination as she tried to count all the bubbles appearing in the batter. He didn't want the moment to end.

He slid the spatula under the pancake and told her to hold on. "One, two…three!"

They flipped it together. A perfect golden brown, the bottom glistening with butter.

Then, Hank's phone rang.

He stayed frozen in place, listening to it chime in the bedroom where it was plugged into the charger.

Evie's head was turned toward it as well, her eyes shining with worry. He knew she was used to phone calls heralding bad news. They were always opportunities for their time together to be split apart; for him to go to work on an expected day off. For Melissa to call and upset the morning—

Gerard's voice echoed through Hank's thoughts at that moment. *"We have to live in the here and now, don't we? We have to stay in the present."*

"Daddy, your phone is ringing," Evie said. Quiet. Sullen.

"I don't hear anything." He winked. "You sure you heard it?"

The ringing stopped as the voicemail picked up.

Evie smiled. "Nope."

They kept making pancakes.

NOTCH ROAD

10:30 A.M.
SUNDAY

Gerard Castle listened to Hank's phone go to voicemail, his breath shuddering. "Good for you, Hank," he muttered. He kept his eyes down on the steering wheel in front of him. If he looked up through the windshield, he'd see the Notch Road pummeled by rain, a dark snake that slid through the pale orange deciduous of the White Mountains in November. He would see the avenue to a potential escape, a way for him to turn back and either go to his lonely, fire-warmed cabin or into town where people and life awaited him.

But he couldn't. He needed to know.

The beep for Hank's voicemail blipped in his ear and Castle coughed to clear his throat before speaking.

When he'd finished his message, he pushed the phone down into his coat pocket, pulled the hood of his rain jacket up over his head and then got out of the car. Rain scattered across his head and shoulders, the smacking loud in his ears. Errant flecks of water hit the lenses of his glasses and a cool gust folded down over him. Finding the most even path to follow down the embankment, Castle meandered across the rocks down to the forest's edge and stepped across the threshold into the trees there.

ANNE'S DINER

1:15 PM
SUNDAY

Hank held Evie's hands and lifted her out of the puddle she'd jumped in. Her laugh was infectious. He couldn't help but lose control of his own as he spun her around and set her down on the sidewalk outside of their favorite diner on the main street of Cardend.

Tromping inside, Hank waved to the owner, Anne, as he and Evie walked down to a booth at the end of the room: their usual table. Taking one sleeve of Evie's polka dot raincoat, Hank helped her take it off. She slid onto one of the overstuffed vinyl red cushions and he dropped down onto the bench opposite her.

As he yanked his own rain jacket off, his phone tumbled from his pocket onto the seat next to him. The screen lit up and a message appeared telling him he'd missed a call and someone had left a voicemail. The missed call was from Gerard.

Hank deflated a little upon seeing it. He hadn't even

checked the missed call that morning, his fear about it being Melissa keeping him from doing so. As Anne stopped by their table with their menus, Hank's hunger dwindled under sudden guilt.

"You two having your usuals: cherry pie, a coffee, and a cocoa?" Anne asked, grabbing the pen from over her ear and clicking it open.

"I want ice cream!" Evie chirped, patting the table excitedly. "Daddy? Ice cream!"

Hank stared at his phone. Why would Gerard have called him this early on a Sunday? Unless he wanted to talk more about last night. Unless he wanted to get something off his chest about their encounter in the woods two weeks ago—

"Daddy!"

He looked up.

Evie huffed impatiently across from him. "I want ice cream. Can I have chocolate ice cream instead of pie?"

"Sure, Eves," he answered, setting the phone aside. "Chocolate explosion, here we come."

Anne jotted down the order and fished into her apron, coming up with a box of crayons which she handed to Evie. As the girl plucked a purple crayon from the box and started coloring in the cartoon bear on the paper place mat before her, Anne leaned over to Hank. "Hank, you feeling okay?"

He struggled to swallow the lump in his throat. A feeling coated his skin like oil then, the feeling that something was wrong. The feeling that he'd missed something, that he hadn't been paying attention when he should have been… "I'm just distracted," he murmured to Anne. "I've got a lot on my mind right now."

Her eyebrows knit together as she regarded him.

Anne had always reminded him of his own mother. She was a woman whose kids had grown up and moved away from the small town of Cardend, embraced the city culture and larger lifestyles of the big cities. Occasionally, they'd all come back to visit and Hank saw that Anne's careful, nurturing influence had rubbed off on each and every one of them. And when she didn't have her own children to look after, she took care of her patrons at the diner with the same kind of motherly devotion. Each cup of coffee, each pancake, each slice of pie was a gift of tenderness delivered in her hands.

"You're a single dad. You're already a superhero, Hank. But you have to take care of yourself, too."

She walked back to the counter and Hank stared at his empty hands on the table. A moment later, she brought back a steaming diner mug of coffee, a small pitcher of cream and a mug of cocoa topped with a spiral of whipped cream, for Evie.

His daughter's eyes grew to the size of dinner plates as she inspected her treat. She mumbled something to herself.

"What, Eves?"

"It's so beautiful."

His anxiety lifted off him and fluttered away.

Reaching down, he tipped the cream into the coffee and then drank from the mug. It warmed him, soothing the chill of the rain, banishing the shadows into the depths of his head. Yes, he had missed Gerard's call.

He could call him later. Gerard knew Sundays were his special day with Evie. He knew their time was precious enough as it was without it being sniped from them by his job or Melissa. He wanted to savor this, too.

He tucked the phone away back into his jacket pocket once more.

RANGER STATION

5:45 PM
SUNDAY

Hank meandered the Jeep along the dirt road, switch-backing through the tall evergreens. The rain had turned to a light snow, which made traveling trickier. There was enough snow to hide a number of potholes; places where if Hank hit them going too fast, he'd potentially slide into a ditch. He didn't have studded snow tires on yet.

He drove slowly, his mind lingering on what had happened at Melissa's.

Nothing had happened. No fighting. No name-calling. No exchange of words at all. Melissa waited on her front stoop; her body protected from the snow under the door canopy. She smoked: he couldn't tell from the Jeep if it was weed or a regular cigarette. She'd started after he and Evie moved out.

The door latch had popped under his fingers as Hank opened the driver's side door and climbed out into the elements. Rounding the car, Hank opened Evie's door and helped her out of the cab. After what felt like too short of a hug and a kiss on her cheek, his daughter ran across the sopping ground to meet her mom.

Melissa didn't make eye contact with him once.

The entire drive to the ranger station, Hank felt like air: unseen and taking up no space. How had things come to this in their marriage? How had they fallen so far from being a family who used to be so close, who used to play board games every Friday night? Who used to go out for pizza at McLeod's and catch a nostalgic movie at the in-town theater?. They must have played Shrek half a dozen times over the last couple years and every time Evie had wanted to go, they'd submitted to defeat.

The lights for the ranger station emitted a soft candle-like glow through the gray gloom of the woods. Hank sighed. As he pulled up alongside some of the other Jeeps in the dirt parking lot and shifted into park, he realized that normal had never been a part of the Feld family dynamic.

Melissa's addiction had always been there, even on the most usual of days. When they would play board games and she hadn't been paying attention at how to play after he'd read all the rules aloud, or when she wouldn't be hungry for pizza at McLeod's. Even at the movie theater when she would take a bit too long coming back from the bathroom during the show...

She'd been using the whole time and he'd ignored the signs until it was too late.

Hank shut off the car and listened to the engine tick as cold bloomed in the once warm space around him. The clock on his dash told him he was only minutes away from his shift beginning. He climbed out into the snow.

Flakes landed and instantly melted on his hair and face as he moved toward the station. Lingering dead leaves and sticks crunched under his boots as he crossed the lot to the steps that led up to the front doors. The smell of the woods pervaded his thoughts: the scent of woodsmoke and evergreen.

Hank pushed through the glass front doors into the main room. The bare wooden accents welcomed him. The white walls displayed old watercolors of the mountains. Though he looked at them almost every day, they brought him comfort; brought him more of that normalcy that he needed. His boots scuffed on the carpet as he took a few steps in and let the door close noiselessly behind him.

Dan stood at the granite front desk talking to Maggie. They were both laughing when he walked through the door.

"Hey, Hank is here," Dan said, giving Maggie a wink. "Guess that means my shift is up." He plodded down the hallway toward his office, most likely to grab his coat and bag.

Maggie shook her head and greeted Hank with a warm smile that gradually thawed as she took in his demeanor. "You okay there, buddy?"

"Yeah," Hank said, instinct powering his voice. "It's always hard saying goodbye to Evie on Sundays, you know?"

It did choke him up: the thought of her being away from him for the whole night into the next day. He'd see her again after his shift ended but he was supposed to pull a double tonight because of poor staffing. They'd had issues with it for a while after the summer ended. The attention their little town had gotten in the last couple weeks because of the bear attack had not helped in their quest for new employees either.

It meant he wasn't getting out until tomorrow night.

He wouldn't see Evie until it was dark again.

Maggie clicked her tongue and brushed a dark curl away from her face. "Why don't you get settled in? Get yourself a cup of coffee and come help me go over digitizing these logs."

Hank nodded and proceeded down the hall to the break room. He hung his jacket on a hook opposite the time clock and pulled his phone out. The voicemail message from Gerard still displayed on the screen. He'd gone the entire day without listening to it. And since that morning, Gerard hadn't attempted to try and reach him again.

Thumbing down the play button, he put the phone to his ear and listened.

"You asked me what I saw up there at Shimmering Rock," Gerard said, his tone pensive. "I saw my son. I saw David. I've seen him since then, too. I thought it was my imagination, thought it was my mind playing tricks on me but… I really think he's here. And I have to know, Hank. I have to know why." He sighed. "Please call me back. Try and talk me out of it." He hung up.

Hank's mind reeled. He quickly played the message again, plugging his other ear with a finger to make sure he was hearing everything that Gerard had said correctly.

Dan bustled into the room, opening the fridge and grabbing a half-empty bottle of orange soda. He glanced at Hank out of the corner of his eyes warily.

"…I have to know, Hank. I have to know why… Please call me back. Try and talk me out of it."

Click.

"Hank?"

Hank looked up at Dan.

"What's up?" his boss asked.

Hank cleared his throat. "I have a bad feeling about something." He tried calling Gerard back. The phone rang.

And rang.

And rang.

"Is something going on with Evie?" Dan asked.

Hank hung up the phone. His throat was tight, his thoughts spinning as he tried to make sense of Gerard's message. "When's the last time anyone saw Gerard Castle?"

Dan's expression firmed. "Last night. He was at the bar with you, remember?"

"You didn't see him today? No one spotted him in town today?"

Dan shook his head. "I've been here since seven a.m. I don't think I've gotten any calls about him but I'm not sure why I would. You want to tell me what's going on?"

Hank stuffed the phone in his pocket. "We need to go find him. Now."

Dan held up his keys. "I'll drive."

THE NOTCH ROAD

6:35 P.M.

Hank was simultaneously grateful and sick to his stomach that Dan had volunteered to drive them to Gerard's cabin out on the Notch Road. Had Hank decided to get behind the wheel, there was a very real chance that he'd have sped: an act that wasn't entirely safe in the current weather conditions. The snow had turned back to rain the further down the mountain they'd driven. Whatever had collected on the roadways had turned to slush, making the road slick.

Dan took each turn with the utmost care. His truck was leased, new by only a month or so and that meant he wasn't about to put it in harm's way in the inclement weather.

The whole drive down, Hank caught Dan up to speed on the voicemail message that Gerard had left as well as the history with Gerard's son, David. David had died in a motorcycle crash a year prior. His body had been found in the woods down a steep embankment where the bike had gone off-road.

As it turned out, Dan recognized the story. His best friend, and their fellow workmate, Andy, had been one of the Search and Rescue team members who had responded to that accident and had talked about it for at least a week afterward. Apparently, the sight of the body had really messed with Andy, who, for all intents and purposes, was the hardest person to make uncomfortable that Dan had ever met.

The mountains could barely be glimpsed through the deluge as night poured in. They stood like steel clouds behind the haze, their presences immense and timeless, towering over the winding roads and whisper-like trees. Hank begged for the rain to lighten up; begged for the darkness to recede if only a little bit.

The turn for Gerard's cabin came and Hank motioned to it as Dan eased the truck onto the wiry dirt lane.

It had to have been a fluke. Maybe Gerard was just having a bad day. Maybe he'd spent the day out in the mountains collecting and charting his moss statistics and then had gone back to his cabin for silence; for reflection and quiet.

But as the truck headlights illuminated the one-story bucolic cabin and its charming front porch, Hank's hopes fizzled. The windows were unlit and no smoke curled from the chimney into the navy sky.

Gerard wasn't there.

Dan shifted into park and exhaled. "Maybe he's at the Howling Owl or over at Anne's?"

Hank frowned. "Anne's is closed by now. I was there today around lunch time and didn't see him like I usually do."

Dan plucked his cell phone from the cup holder beside him. "I'll give Andy a call. I'll bet he's probably already at the bar."

Hank nodded. "I'm going to get out and look around."

Dan waved him on.

Climbing out of the truck, Hank shivered as the rain instantly drenched him. He raced for the covered front porch of Gerard's cabin and only once he was safely under did he take a breath.

Gerard had invited him over a couple days after their near-death experience in the mountains. Hank had left Cardend Memorial that evening. The headaches from his concussion were getting worse and his doctor had set him up with a new prescription to help him sleep.

But Hank was afraid to go back to his apartment that night; was afraid to close his eyes if only for his nightmares to take hold. Since Evie was staying with Melissa that evening, he'd journeyed out to his friend's cabin and they'd spent several hours sitting on the front porch sipping whiskey.

Hank regarded the two rocking chairs nearby where they'd sat and talked about the things they'd left behind; the things they'd thought they had come to terms with.

The truck door slammed and Hank looked up to catch Dan jogging toward him with his jacket held up over his head.

"Andy hasn't seen him," his boss informed, pounding

up onto the deck and flinging his coat back down onto his shoulders. "I told him to meet us up here."

"Gerard isn't here," Hank said.

Dan pointed to the door. "Maybe he left something inside? Something that tells us where he's gone?"

"That's breaking and entering."

"That's just cause," Dan argued. "And we're not fucking *Law and Order* here. He's your friend."

The white noise of the rain washed in and out of Hank's ears. He reached for the door handle and paused. The door was already open a crack. The cold breath of the cabin inside tingled on his fingers as he pushed the door the rest of the way in.

Dan clicked on a flashlight behind him and the light swept into the dark like a cat into the shadows to play.

The cabin opened into a living room with a cast iron wood stove huddled against the right wall beneath a brick chimney. A sleeper sofa and two periwinkle armchairs crowded the small space with a skinny coffee table filling the area between them. The room behind was a small bedroom with a full-sized bed dressed in a pastel quilt. The window there looked out on the river behind the house; its current white and roaring.

The kitchen stood off to the left. Hank and Dan struggled to fit into the tiny space: Hank told Dan where to direct the light and then, frustrated, turned on his own phone's flashlight to investigate for himself.

Hank swept the light over photos on the fridge, a family portrait from decades ago that showed Gerard with, presumably, his wife, Penny, and their son, David, when he was a teenager. The young man shared his father's string bean figure, his height, his narrow eyes and strong chin. He had Penny's nose and her hair.

The punch in his gut from Gerard's phone call caught him again.

"I saw my son. I saw David."

"What did you mean, Gerry?" Hank muttered to himself.

"Hey, Hank?"

Hank half-turned, trying to look over his shoulder at where Dan stood behind him. "What did you find?"

"There's a map here on the table."

"What?" Hank spun around, his boots squeaking as he came up behind Dan and looked over his shoulder at it. The map was waterproof and showed elevation and trails over The White Mountains in interconnected green and red paths.

Dan dropped his finger on a red circle drawn over an area of the forest. "He's got this area marked here."

"Could just be work for his bryology studies…" Hank thought aloud. "But…"

The area Gerard had circled was directly off of the Notch Road, a few miles further down the mountain from where they currently were. "No. I think I know what this is."

"I've seen him since then, too."

"Where?"

"This is where his son died. It's where they found his body." Saying it out loud sent spikes of ice down through him. The skin on his arms and legs prickled.

Dan squinted. "Why would he mark it on a map and

not take it with him though?"

Hank reached down and picked it up, carefully folding it. "Because the map wasn't for him: it's for me. It's why he left the cabin door open, too. He's gone there and he wants me to find him."

THE NOTCH ROAD

8:15 PM

Dan and Hank met Andy at a hiking trail parking lot up the road from the place Gerard Castle had circled on his map. David Castle had died when his bike went into a guardrail and down into a ravine near the forest's edge. In the dark and in the rain, they had all made a decision to not to traverse the steep decline. It was too dangerous. The temperature was flirting with freezing again and that meant there was potential for all of that rain to ice up. They couldn't afford to twist an ankle.

They'd gone back to the ranger station to collect supplies for the last-minute hike into the woods. Hank was insistent they head out as soon as possible, while they had a fresh lead. It had been less than twenty-four hours after Gerard had disappeared. If he was out in the woods in this kind of weather, the chances of him catching hypothermia were severe. If Gerard died, Hank would never forgive himself for not picking up the phone that morning.

"You sure you're good?" Dan asked Andy as the latter hauled his backpack out of the passenger side of his truck and slung it on.

"I'm not sloshed, Dan," Andy rebuked, clipping the sternum strap and tightening it a little. "Hadn't even taken a sip of my beer when you called. Though it would have made a more fun trip for all of us, I think." When Hank gave him a side-eye, Andy blew a raspberry at him. "Kidding. Obviously."

"He's been out there for ten hours at maximum," Dan said, cinching the waist belt on his pack to tighten it. "I'm hoping that when the weather turned, Gerard searched for a place to take cover. There's no huts in this area of the valley but there is an old kiosk at the tail end of Wingbeat Trail."

"Wingbeat?" Hank shook his head. "I don't know that one."

"It used to connect the Dry River Trail to Mount Resolution." Dan reached into his truck and grabbed his headlamp from the cup holder before fitting it on his head. When he turned it on, it blinded Hank. He looked away and subsequently blinded Andy. "Sorry. The trail got pretty thrashed with downed trees and erosion and eventually, we had to close it. It just wasn't safe anymore."

"Any idea what kind of shape it's in now?" Hank asked, blinking to lose the spots that now danced in his vision. He secured his own pack and adjusted the load-lifting straps. The sheer nostalgia of a couple weeks ago took him off-guard suddenly. Getting his pack ready to head up the mountain to go save those kids, hiking in the cold with thin air, Gerard lagging behind as their route grew more and more vertical…

Dan had been talking and Hank hadn't caught half of what he'd said. He forced himself to pay attention to Dan's next words. "…won't be a great. But the eastern side of the trail is in decent shape. If we can find him and get all of us out of there before temperatures drop below freezing, we might have a chance."

Andy clapped his hands. "The night is young! Let's go find a hallucinating old guy!"

"Andy…" Dan reproved.

The three of them crossed the dirt parking lot until the shelter of the woods drew them in. Hank stared into the white pall provided by his headlamp as it lit up Dan's back and tried to measure his breaths; to keep his muscles taut but not strained.

Sticks crackled under the men's boots as they meandered down the trail, skirting frosty rocks and slick roots. All the while, the forest watched them in near perfect silence. Water dripped from the branches of the ancient trees. The men grunted and huffed as they adjusted to the cold.

Hank thought about the woods. He thought about launching into them two weeks ago in search of Gina and her friends. He thought about finding one of their bodies on the exposed ridge. The sight had made him sick then and haunted him now: the unnatural greyness of the skin, the torn eye sockets and shredded remains where his legs had been…

The gurgle of a river reached out to him seconds before another sound split the night: the shrill cry of an animal.

Hank froze. His heart was in his throat and he couldn't swallow it, its steady beat drumming harder and harder.

"Fisher cat," Andy said. He danced his flashlight beam between a couple trees on the edge of the river. "Sounds like a woman shrieking for her life. Fucking awful, isn't it?"

Hank had heard fisher cats before: their banshee-like calls keening over the forest as he'd huddled in lean-tos and tried to coax sleep forward. This unnerved him; like a live wire attached to his nervous system. He wanted to believe Andy. At the same time, he searched his memory for how that monster had sounded a couple weeks ago on the ridge. It was a sound he'd thought he'd never forget.

As the scream muddled his thoughts, Hank realized a lot of what he thought he remembered from that night wasn't as sharp now. There were so many shadows on that Halloween night in the dense forest. He'd hidden for so much of it, not to mention he'd hit his head at one point. Maybe he'd filled in blanks with assumptions after all. Maybe the concussion was making it hard to rememb—

"Watch it!"

Hank was in mid-step when he felt Andy's hand slap across his chest. Back in the here and now, Hank stared at a sheer drop off before him. The rocks below shimmered with ice beneath the glare of the headlamp.

Dan came up on his other side and gave him a stern

look. "Get out of your head. Pay attention. We can't lose you out here, too." Then, he continued toward the trail's gentle decline off to the left.

Stay focused, Hank reminded himself before following after his boss. Andy took up the rear.

"Listen," Andy said under his breath. "I get that you're worried. But Gerard has experience hiking in the woods, right? He was probably smart enough to find a place to hole up."

"Unless that's not what he came out here to do," Hank said aloud without meaning to. The thought had skirted around the edges of his brain ever since listening to Gerard's message. He'd never thought his friend was the type to end his own life, but Gerard's attitude the night before at The Howling Owl strengthened the idea the longer Hank mulled on it.

"We have to be prepared for that, too," Andy added, his tone decidedly casual in spite of the topic. "Whatever happens, you have to just…c'est la vie it."

"Ah, French motivational inspiration," Dan said over his shoulder. "I think you've been spending too much time with Trey…that Canadian bastard."

Hank glanced back to catch Andy shrugging. "Ooh, sensitive tonight, aren't we?"

They reached the bottom of the drop off and came to an old route marker pinned to one of the nearby trees. Two pieces of wood with arrows pointing in opposite directions were screwed into the bark just above their heads. The one to the right marked a continuation of the Hatchling Spring Trail while the one to the left was carved to show Wingbeat Trail. The trail head was blocked off with a chain and a flag marking the route was now closed.

"There's a chance he could have continued on the Hatchling Spring Trail," Dan said before turning back to Hank and Andy. "I'm going to take this one. I want you two to take Wingbeat. Turn to channel two on your radios. If you find something, let me know."

"You gonna be okay out there on your own?" Hank asked, eying the trail to the right. It curled down through the trees following the river and vanished.

Dan gave a wistful smile. "To be honest, I'd rather be home with Alicia enjoying the pizza she picked up from McLeod's. But I'm sure I'll survive."

"Well, pizza's only going to make you fat anyway," Andy buzzed, chuckling to himself. "We'll be in touch."

After flipping Andy off, Dan sidled off down the Hatchling Spring Trail; his pack shuffling against his jacket.

Andy stepped one of his long legs over the chain at Wingbeat Trail and after crossing, held it up for Hank to crouch under. They started down the overgrown path.

HATCHLING SPRING TRAIL

10:45 A.M.
SUNDAY MORNING

Trepidation was the tickle of a hundred ants crawling on Gerard's skin. From the moment he set foot in the Woods, all he could think about was seeing David again. All he could picture was hugging his son, kissing his hair, telling him how much he missed him... But behind those desires, rationality stung and kept him grounded.

David was *dead*. He had died over a year ago. He had been riding his motorcycle on a night where the roads were slick and was going too fast.

Gerard should have called him and told him not to come that night; to wait until the weather eased. But he'd been selfish. He'd wanted to spend time with his son and that weekend was going to be just the two of them: drinking beers, fishing at the stream behind the house, catching up... He'd wanted to ask him a thing or two about how his work was going, who was he dating, had he thought about buying a house yet...

Some of the questions had been Penny's. She'd sent Gerard with a volley of them; knew he was more likely to extract answers from their son than she was. But Gerard had been curious about David's answers as well. He'd been in touch less and less after getting his new job in Boston and while it wasn't too far from their home in Connecticut, he wished, like all parents, that David had chosen a city just a little closer to live in.

The underbrush crackled in front of Gerard and he stiffened. His hand sprung to his fanny pack zipper. He'd brought bear spray in case he came across the horrible monster that had killed those teens on the ridge weeks ago. Even though it had been reported as a bear, deep down, Gerard knew it wasn't and that bear spray would do little to save him if he ran into the thing.

Something small zipped from the dried ferns in front of him and scuttled up a nearby tree. Gerard chuckled as the shiny black eyes of a red squirrel stared at him from the crook of two branches. It chittered.

"You scared me, too," Gerard muttered, shaking his head.

When he brought his head back up, a person stood in the weeds where there had previously been none. He practically choked as the air left him for a moment. As the figure drew a few steps closer, cold seared Gerard's cheeks.

David regarded him with distant warmth. Gerard recognized the black leather jacket his son had worn often on the bike, the old Guns n' Roses t-shirt and his weathered-looking boots peeking out from under worn jeans. He seemed taller since Gerard had last seen him when they'd gotten together last Easter, a realization that made tears singe at the corners of his eyes. David had been wearing all of this when he'd died.

David was the first to speak. "Dad."

Gerard opened his mouth and couldn't find his voice.

His son gave a shy smile. "First time you've ever had trouble coming up with something to say."

Gerard cleared his throat. "I just…can't believe it. You're here." His legs twitched with the desperate desire to cross the distance between them; to pull his son close and never let him go. Just as the feeling got the better of him, David put up a hand.

"You can't."

Gerard's throat swelled. "Why not?"

David tentatively reached out a hand. "Go ahead. Try."

Nostrils flaring, Gerard extended his fingers. Upon reaching David's hand, his own was instantly dredged in a cold unlike any other he'd experienced. His skin burned as he yanked it back and gasped. "What the hell?" he murmured, shaking it. "What the…"

"See what I mean?" David said.

The disappointment at not being able to touch David was dowsed with frustration. "How are you here? How is this happening?"

David merely shrugged.

"Was this because of what those kids did up on Shimmering Rock? That séance?" He felt stupid asking the question. Seances were old parlor tricks. Ouija boards were children's games. Whatever had attacked and killed those kids two weeks ago on the ridge was flesh and bone even if he had been convinced of the contrary moments ago.

"I think the Woods were there before that ever happened," David said, though he didn't sound so sure. "Those kids were just in the wrong place at the wrong time."

"What do you mean 'the Woods?'" Gerard asked. As he did, his eyes flickered to his surroundings. The woods around them didn't feel any different than the ones he'd spent his whole career and even retirement studying. Granted, he'd only been to this particular place once and it was upon hearing about David's death. Hell, he hadn't studied this section of the White Mountains National Forest at all. It wasn't on his list of trails to set up samples at.

Yet, like the rest of the forest he knew, he recognized each variant of tree and plant that sprung up around him, noted the various forms of moss and lichen like they were old friends as he'd journeyed through the forest. Nothing was out of the ordinary here. Nothing except for David.

"I'll show you," David said, and started to turn around. After taking only one step, he turned back. "You have to stay quiet though. It's dangerous if you don't."

Gerard swallowed. He wasn't much of a silent observer. He'd always been the student who asked too many questions during labs, who always wanted a closer look at things, who encouraged conversation and discussion and loved idle chat.

But the severity on David's face now had his mind swimming in anxiety. Where were they going? Gerard barely made himself nod and his jaw tightened for fear that if he said "no", David would walk into the forest and vanish, never to be seen again.

Gerard dipped under an old chain for a trail that wasn't in use anymore and followed his son further into the woods.

WINGBEAT TRAIL

8:45 P.M.
SUNDAY NIGHT

"What's the matter?" Castle had asked Hank the night he'd shown up for beers at the former's cabin.

"I'm tired, Gerry. I'm tired of trying," Hank had answered. He'd forced himself to say those words when in reality, all he'd wanted to do was cry.

It was day in and day out of the same misery with Melissa, the same testing from Evie as she pushed at his thinning band of heartache. When he'd tried to put her to bed the night before, she'd gotten upset because of some story she wanted him to read; a story from a book that her mother had at her house that Hank didn't. When he'd tried to tell different one, Evie had cried and said he was ruining everything. She'd sobbed for her mom and he'd felt powerless.

Gerard had leaned forward in his rocking chair and threaded his fingers together around his beer bottle. He squinted behind his square-framed glasses as he said,

"Trying is hard. You do an amazing amount of trying, Hank. It may not feel like it but you're succeeding."

"Am I?" Hank's voice had cracked a little and he'd cleared his throat to keep it steady. "I don't know. I could have died out here last week searching for those kids on the mountain. Evie wouldn't have understood and she'd have felt…abandoned."

Gerard inhaled. "Stop, stop, stop… Listen. Look at me."

Hank had. The sternness in his friend's eyes brought his fears to a grinding halt.

"You are here. You are *here*. So, do the best you can do for her and for you. That's all you can—"

Andy bumped Hank with his elbow. "What did one sparrow say to the other sparrow? 'Leave me the flock alone.'"

Hank exhaled, pushing the stress and the despair from him in one stale breath before pulling in a new one. The night had turned crisp and bit at his cheeks. He pulled the hood of his puffy jacket up over his head under the rain shell to try and insulate himself from the deepening cold.

"Well, you didn't laugh at that joke either, so I guess you're not really listening, are you?" Andy added, staring down at Hank.

"Maybe you're just not as funny as you think you are." Hank's tone had an edge to it.

Andy cocked his head. "You know, for someone searching for a lost friend, you've been incredibly quiet. You haven't called his name at all in the last ten minutes we've been walking."

Hank said nothing. While he'd been aware of their surroundings enough to make sure he didn't take a nosedive off a steep embankment, Hank had been stuck reminiscing. It was hard to tear himself out of it once he started. He'd been doing that more than usual since his concussion.

Over the last two weeks, he'd caught himself sitting at a stoplight only for the cars behind him to start honking because he didn't notice the light turn green. He'd burned several of the things he'd cooked. He'd even forgotten where his keys and phone were several mornings.

The doctor had told him it would pass. Hank *needed* it to pass sooner rather than later now.

"You know what I'm going to say," Andy said. "You know what Dan would say."

"I can't leave him out here," Hank answered. "What the hell kind of friend would I be?"

Andy frowned. "Gerard knows how good of a friend you are. But if you're not one hundred percent here right now, Hank, you pose a risk; not just to me but to yourself and to Gerard. You know all of this."

He did. He was compromised. He should have gone back.

As Hank started to talk, their radios chirped to life.

"Andy? Hank? You there, over?" Dan's voice echoed through the speaker.

Andy was quick to answer in a mock French accent. "Bonjour, Monsieur Cooper! Monsieur Feld and I are standing by, over."

"Knock it off, Andy. I've got a lost hiker out here about a quarter mile off the Hatchling Spring Trail. Caucasian woman in her mid-thirties. Seems to have rolled an ankle, maybe injured her knee as well. She told me her friend was supposed to have gone back to the car for help but that was hours ago. I need you to double back to my location and help me get her safely to the parking lot. I've already called in an ambulance. Over."

"Ten-four, buddy. We'll be there soon. Over and out." Andy clicked the radio onto his belt and turned back the way they'd come. There was resignation in his blue eyes. "We'll have to try again in a little bit once we've called in for some back up, Hank."

Panic nested in Hank's chest. "No."

"No, what?"

"You know as well as I do that Dan doesn't need both of us. I'll stay and keep looking for Gerard myself."

Andy scoffed. "No offense, you can't be trusted out here on your own right now. You might walk off another cliff like Mr. Magoo."

"You know what happens if we stop searching right now. It takes us at least another hour to get that other hiker back to the parking lot, another half to fill in some more search and rescue members, to get the paramedics up to speed... By the time we get back out here, it's after midnight and the temps will be below freezing."

Andy scratched at his jaw. "This is dumb, Hank. What if I leave you and something happens?"

"I told you I wasn't laughing because your jokes were bad, not because I wasn't paying attention. I can still radio for back up. I still have my GPS that I can send a signal from in case you don't hear from me. I've got enough supplies to last a night out here if need be."

When Andy didn't say anything, Hank pressed. "We are *wasting* time."

An owl called across the forest. It seemed to get quieter in its wake.

"Shit," Andy muttered and unbuckled his hip and shoulder straps to sling his pack off. He unzipped the brain of his bag, pulled out an emergency flare, and handed it to Hank. "No bullshit. If you find him and can't get him out of here on your own, you radio me. If you get in over your head, you use this flare and you still radio me. Capiche?"

"You've got it," Hank said, taking the flare.

Andy secured his pack once more and started back toward the main trail. He stopped and looked over his shoulder hesitantly, "Two hallucinating men walk into a bar…"

Hank waved at him. "Get."

Andy jerked his head back a little. "Fine. The joke felt applicable, that's all." Within a few moments, his footfalls died off. Hank was once again surrounded by silence.

WINGBEAT TRAIL

11:00 A.M.

Castle followed his son through the weeds for fifteen minutes, the only sound being his own footfalls. He watched as David's legs blurred and blended around the foliage in the hazy light. Every time he focused on it, he started to feel a bit lightheaded and distant. He pinched himself hard between his thumb and forefinger, desperate to ground himself. He even thought about giving his own cheek a slap for good measure.

He'd never had a dream like this before: a dream where he was in control of everything happening; a dream where he could smell and touch and hear everything in perfect synchronization. But this wasn't a dream. He had to keep telling himself that. David was there a few steps ahead of him, leading him deeper and deeper into, well… Gerard wasn't quite sure.

As they'd walked, the light faded and the air grew humid. Gerard peeled off his rain shell when the temperature became too stifling to keep it on. This was ridiculous. It was late November in the Whites; it wasn't supposed to be this hot here. There was supposed to be snow and, if not that, at least frost. His hands should have been red and shaking without gloves. He was sure the weather had even called for snow showers that evening.

A warm front? Here? No. No, no, no, no.

Gerard looked up and noticed that David had stopped and was staring back at him expectantly. "It's just up ahead."

"What's 'just up ahead' exactly?" Gerard asked.

"The place that brought me here," David said, moving effortlessly through a large gathering of ferns. "The place that monster came from that attacked those kids…"

"You're not making any sense, David. A *place* brought you here? From where?"

"I told you." David waved his hand. "It's just up ahead." He turned and kept going.

A queasiness settled in Gerard's stomach as he made himself continue after his son. What if this wasn't David after all? God, what if he was hallucinating?

Dementia was in his family. While his own father had died from alcoholism, his mother had suffered a steady cognitive decline in her old age, something that had killed Gerard to watch happen. She'd been brilliant. Her work and love of the forest had pushed him to pursue biological studies, too. And by the end, she'd needed to be spoon-fed at a hospice center.

As Gerard mulled his fears over, he shuffled around the ferns and stepped back onto a clear section of the old trail. An oppressive warmth blanketed him as he fixed his sights on David's back and then, the presence before them both. Gerard's mouth opened and he tilted his head back, forcing himself to breathe. "Oh, God."

The trees looked like black paint dripped from the gray canvas of sky. Their dark forms bled into a fog-saturated expanse before them. The dripping woods stood on the edge of the forest that Gerard recognized, and everything beyond them was shielded by a gloom of shadow.

"These are the Woods," David said, his tone vacant, reverent. "This is where I woke up after I…" He didn't say anything more.

Gerard wasn't sure what David meant but he could guess and the guess filled his stomach with knots. This was where David had gone after he'd died, where his ghost had appeared. But why? Why had this place held onto him? Why hadn't he…moved on?

The pitch was steep there: the assumption of an afterlife, of something that awaited him; them; everyone after death. Gerard had grown up with the typical western religion diatribe from his parents since he was young. He'd been forced to dress up and go to church, participate in Sunday school until he and some friends ran off to be roadies for Bob Dylan out of high school. Only then, had he had a fresh perspective: his own. He'd had time to analyze how much of faith was spirituality and whether or not that was something he shared with countless others.

He hadn't, not for a long time, not until David's death.

Penny had been the crack in his methodical beliefs. Her want to believe in something for the sake of their son had pushed him into a flurry of passing thoughts that usually hit him just before falling asleep or waking up.

But maybe *this* was what came after. Maybe the scales had tipped and sent all the spirits spilling back down onto earth, along with the wretched purgatory they ended up in?

"Hey, Dad?"

Gerard took a deep and sudden breath. "It's, uh, a lot to take in."

"I understand. I didn't take it any easier," David said.

"Why did you want to show me this, son?"

David frowned. "I'm not sure. Maybe because I thought you'd want to know."

Gerard felt himself backing away from the darkness.

"Dad?"

Gerard hadn't wanted to know. He would have been fine if he'd imagined that David had ended up in some typical afterlife scenario: a place with light and goodness, lots of clouds, maybe even some blueberry fields, which David had always liked to hike around when he'd been alive.

The thirst for knowledge that had driven Gerard most of his life had dried up when it came to David's death. While the pain would never go away, at least he'd gotten to a place where he could live with it day to day, where his wife could look at photos on the fridge and not break down in tears automatically, or say his name without her voice cracking.

"Why did you come back now? Why after all this time?" he asked, somehow keeping his voice even.

"You ask like I had some kind of a choice," David said, and Gerard caught the touch of offense in his tone. "Are you not happy to see me?"

The question slid into one of Gerard's lungs like a knife. He took a reflexive breath. "Of course, I am. But it… It hurts, too."

David shared a knowing look. "I'd ask how Mom is but I think I already know."

Gerard swallowed. "She took your death really hard, Davey."

A distant call rose up from somewhere in the trees. Both of them turned toward it. Gerard's skin prickled as he stilled. A voice rang out deep in the Woods in front of them.

"Help!" The voice echoed. "Is anyone out there?"

David's eyes glazed over with fear.

Gerard frowned. "Who is that?" He cupped his hands around his mouth and shouted back, "Is someone in there?"

David put his hands up, his eyes rounded. "Stop! Dad, stop!"

"Hello?" the voice called back in their direction.

Gerard narrowed his gaze at David. "What's wrong with you? Someone is lost out here. We have to help them."

"You need to be quiet, Dad," David hissed, crouching in the ferns. Their fronds blended with his figure and left smoky tracks as they swished back and forth.

"This isn't how I raised you," Gerard said, his hand instinctively going for the pocket of his fanny pack. "You can't just ignore—"

A snarl trundled over the fog from deep within the trees. It was distant but the dread it ushered forth in Gerard's body was like a tide steadily rolling in. He recognized it from that night in the woods: that night with Gina.

David reached for Gerard. "We have to run, have to hide… We need to go. Now!"

And Gerard reached back without thinking about the sharp cold that awaited him from David's embrace as they both ran.

WINGBEAT TRAIL

9:30 P.M.

A familiar chill wrapped itself around Hank as he came around the next bend in the trail. A darkness loomed ahead that swallowed the light from his headlamp; that drank the rain pouring around him. He stared into a void, tangled with unfamiliar trees and brush.

This must have been the overgrown part of the trail, the one that had been left to the wilderness years ago. Yet, as Hank stared, he couldn't help but remember his experiences on the mountain. Shimmering Rock had been bound in a dark forest very similar to this one, where the darkness felt like a coating on his skin and clothes.

He had parted ways with Andy almost an hour ago. Hank imagined the him helping Dan, and the injured hiker they found, out to the parking lot where an ambulance likely waited. He'd hoped he'd have heard from one of them by now, if only to plant a stake in the idea that he wasn't completely alone out here in this section of the Whites.

He'd never worried about being alone in the woods before. Hank's entire career as a park ranger was based around his teenage ideology of breaking out on his own, of escaping the city where he'd grown up and embracing the solitude that the outdoors could bring.

Never could he have imagined as a stocky, sheltered kid that a summer job volunteering for one of the huts would have turned into a lifelong passion to protect and patrol these mountains. But, all of that had changed when he'd found himself huddled in the dark, not breathing as he watched a kid have his soul ripped out of him; a kid who had been the same age as he had when he came out here for the first time. And he couldn't stop imagining himself in place of that kid…

A hollow wail of wind crept out of the trees before him. The warm gust hit his face and brought color back to his cheeks. He frowned. The temperature was supposed to have been in the twenties but here, it felt much warmer than that.

He cupped his hands in front of his mouth. "Gerard!" he yelled into the darkness.

And something called back. But Hank couldn't figure out what. It had sounded like a whimper. Was Gerard hurt? Was it an animal? Or what about that other lost hiker's partner who was supposed to have gone back to the car for help?

"I'm coming," Hank said, more to psyche himself up than as a response to whoever or whatever had made the sound. He pressed forward into the new darkness.

THE WOODS

11:30 A.M.

Gerard wasn't sure where he was going anymore. He wasn't sure where David was. He thought his son ran this way, in the opposite direction of the shriek, somewhere obliquely tunneling off into the thick black trees. But David hadn't made any noise because he'd simply vanished. With all of Gerard's thrashing in the brush, he wasn't sure he could hear David's voice even if he tried to listen for it. He wasn't sure if he could hear anything over the drumming of his own heartbeat and its resounding cacophony in his head.

What Gerard was sure of was that there was someone else lost out there, lost in the Woods with that *thing* that tore those kids apart weeks ago and he was the only other one who knew about it. This recognition slowed him down; made him slip behind the cover of a tree and take deep, patient breaths through his nose, all the while keeping his eyes closed.

The rain had stopped. A moist heat pressed against him, one he recalled from his time doing studies in the rain forest. It was uncomfortable and nearly made his heart rate take off again by its alienness. It didn't belong there. It didn't belong in New Hampshire in November. It didn't belong in the Northeast at all.

"Dad."

Gerard opened his eyes.

David stood before him with a finger to his lips while the other motioned for him to get down low.

Gerard did as instructed. His eyes skipped around to take in his surroundings. This wasn't any place he knew, not the comforting mist-soaked woods of the White Mountains, not the deep, verdant gush of a Central American jungle. This was a woodland dipped in oil; smothered in fog.

Moss-strangled trees towered all around him, their height impossible, as their tops vanished into a gloom of darkness above. He couldn't see the forest floor, even as he knelt down closer to it. It was darker than it should have been at this time of the day, darker than it should have been with the trees spaced as far apart as they were. The only reason he could see David was because his figure was silhouetted by the green vibrancy of the trees around him. It was as if light existed in the distance far off somehow, and its presence was the only reminder of the real world he'd left behind.

Gerard wanted nothing more than to close his eyes and open them to find he'd been having a nightmare. He should have known better than to go searching in the woods where David had died. He'd *died*. This wasn't supposed to happen and he wasn't supposed to be here.

The brush rustled a few feet from them and Gerard saw the shine of his son's eyes as they widened even more.

He searched the darkness for the source of the noise. Each footfall in the leaves made his heart quiver. Something was walking, it's gait steady. As much as Gerard wanted to stay crouched, a much larger curiosity itched right then: the need to know, the need to find answers in spite of how terrified he felt.

As quietly and as slowly as he could manage, Gerard peered around the edge of his son's form up over the foliage.

The blackness beyond him was almost complete, save for the greenness of the trees and a film of light that exuded somewhere in the distance. Then, darkness parted from darkness and Gerard wished he had never looked at all.

The shape was long and agile and moved with the grace of a shadow sliding over the landscape. For seconds, it seemed almost as harmless as one, too. Until he saw its eyes, or the reflection of them against that distant glow: pale and filmy like the full moon. Until he saw the glimmer of teeth like a slash of light.

Almost as soon as he saw it, the shadow was gone.

Gerard squinted into the darkness. Where had it disappeared so fast? He couldn't have lost it that quickly...

But another sound disturbed the near quiet now. More footsteps crackled in the underbrush, much louder than the first ones. These were hurried, stumbling over the landscape. Lost footsteps.

David glanced back over his shoulder, following Gerard's gaze as a figure appeared out of the darkness.

They were jogging, but not lightly. They stopped and braced themselves with hands against knees. They sucked in breaths. Muttering. Cursing. "Fuck. Fuck. Shit."

A steady thundering had begun in Gerard's temples. His heart quickened. This poor person. Did they even know what they'd wandered into? Did they know how close they were to one of those—

"Don't even think about it," David whispered. His voice was as brittle as glass, so unlike the young man Gerard remembered his son being. There was so much fear inside of that voice that Gerard almost forgot what he'd been in the middle of doing. But he'd steadied himself to stand up. He'd started to try and make his way across the forest to that person...

"What if it was your mother?" Gerard said, blankly.

Guilt glazed over David's face.

Gerard's knees shook as he brought himself to a full standing position. God, he hated being old. "What if it was her who was lost out here? Wouldn't you try to help her?"

"It's not," David said, indignantly. "And if it comes down to a stranger's life over yours, you know who I'd pick. Besides, it won't matter."

The person in the distance righted themselves and started walking again.

Gerard wasn't sure he was moving until a few steps had gone by, his brain winning over the terror David had put in his head: the terror that had spiked at seeing whatever that thing was lurking a few moments ago.

David hissed his name from the shadows but didn't come after him.

"Hey!" Gerard called, waving his hands. "Over here!"

The figure swung toward him, their head jerking back and forth to examine the dark woods. "Hello?"

"I'm coming!" A smile broadened on Gerard's lips as he got closer to them. "Stay right there. I'm coming to you."

But as he neared the figure, they suddenly stepped forward, their footsteps confident, their voice carrying them further into the darkness. "Hello!?" they yelled ahead of them as they moved.

"Wait!"

Gerard plodded after them, picking a path over the twisted roots. How had they not heard him? Gerard had never been accused of being quiet in his life and certainly hadn't been whispering when he tried to get that hiker's attention. Maybe they were disoriented? Injured somehow?

"It's not worth it, Dad. Please stop!" David pleaded, off to his left now.

But David's words only lit a fire under Gerard and he plunged further into the dark after the hiker. "Hey! Turn around! I'm right here."

"Where the hell am I?" the person bemoaned, not turning back. "What the hell is this?"

Gerard was convinced: this person must have been severely out of it. Or they were on drugs. Or their bad hearing was amplified by their stress… Whatever the reason, as soon as they saw him, everything would be okay.

But David appeared in front of him and the suddenness of it stopped Gerard dead in his tracks. "You need to stop!" David yelled. "That isn't someone you can help. Not anymore. They're one of the Lost."

The words sunk in to Gerard's brain like teabags, their pervasion staining; drifting tendrils throughout him. "They're…like you?"

He nodded. "And they can't *see* you. Your voice sounds like a distant echo coming from every direction to them."

"But…" Gerard let the word drop off his tongue without meaning to. "How did you hear me in the woods that night? How did you find me today?"

"Because we're not strangers. We're attached." David blinked. "I'd hear you wherever you are, Dad."

"Attached? I'm not sure I understand."

"When I was out here wandering, it was *your* voice that guided me out. I heard you talking to me one of those times you stopped on the roadside where it happened."

Gerard's brows knit. He wasn't sure he could count the number of times he'd spent parked on the Notch Road, monologuing to his memory of David about what life was like without him. It was probably in the hundreds. But it had actually worked. David had actually heard him?

"I couldn't follow it until that night though, in the Woods when you were trying to save those kids. You were closer then. I could almost…feel you."

The words were like impacts. They should have

comforted him. Gerard didn't even feel the ground as he fell to his knees, didn't feel the sting of them nor the warm, wetness of the forest floor. His skin felt like it was dredged in sorrow: one that ebbed deeper the longer he thought about David's words, numbing as it went.

The scream was abrupt and sent barbs through Gerard's deadening sadness. He looked up in time to see the lost soul he'd been trying to save running toward him, the darkness swirling around them. He almost thought he saw their face and the surprised oh of their mouth as something snapped them into the ferns with lightning speed. Their body hammered across the ground with a wretched yelp that made the air in Gerard's lungs evaporate.

They shrieked as their body was dragged further off into the Woods.

Gerard was frozen.

David panted, his whole body tense. "Now, do you get it?" David asked.

Gerard tried to say something but all that came out was a grunt as he picked himself up. He was sopping wet, his clothes damp from perspiration and the earth beneath him, if he could even still call it that. But his mind was seizing; screaming for answers.

"We need to head for the border of the Woods right now." David crept toward the trees from where they had hidden earlier. "I need to get you back to safety."

"W-what about you?" Gerard stammered.

"It's too late for me," David said, looking back at him.

Gerard's face twisted. "No. That can't be true. This

can't be all it is. There has to be something—"

"What?" David interrupted. "Something better? There isn't. At least, I don't think there is." He added the last bit quietly. When he turned back toward the trees, he stopped moving.

"Davey?"

"No," David spoke, his breath tremulous. "No!"

Gerard poked his head to look around David's side.

The hulking shape that rose from the brambles at the forest floor looked nearly the same: a mass parting itself from the other thorns. As the limbs twisted and rose into massive stalks, a hulking shape formed from the blackness.

"Run, Dad! Get—"

David's voice was cut off as the creature launched itself at him, its entire body barreling into his with frightening velocity.

Gerard hit the ground as David's arms and legs trailed across his back. The ensuing touch was like being sliced with an ax. Pain consumed him like biting ants crawling all over his skin.

He retreated into himself: arms and legs curling to protect his chest, ears barely registering the helplessness of his son's cries. The sounds forced his eyes open, teeth clenched as he fought against the receding agony. He needed to get control of his limbs, to make himself turn over.

Not my son! Not David!

But dread held him in place, and while he managed to flip over, he couldn't get himself up off the ground, paralyzed by the scene before him.

The monster stood over David, its muzzle inches away from his face as its opalescent eyes gleamed hideously down at him. In one fluid motion, it gnashed its teeth around the collar of David's jacket and heaved him across the forest floor.

The last thing Gerard heard was David's pleading cries as he shouted back to him. They echoed into the darkness as the thing carried him further away. After a few more moments, silence reigned.

THE WOODS

10:15 PM

The headache had gotten worse. Hank wasn't imagining it. He had pushed himself, trying to ignore it as it slipped in and began writhing across his skull. He was dehydrated. He was hungry. He was also sure the headache wasn't because of either of those two things.

"They tell you to keep taking that stuff for your head?" He remembered Gerard asking the night they'd gotten together on the older man's porch.

"Yeah." Hank closed his eyes for a moment, hoping the pain would abate but it seemed to twinge all the more. When he opened his eyes, he was back on the lightless trail in the woods, far away from Gerard's comfortable cabin.

It took him a moment to remember where he was, to remember where he'd come from. He stopped and glanced into the equally potent dark behind him. He wasn't sure if he was still on the old disused trail anymore or if he'd stepped off of it while not paying attention. There were no trail markers on any of the trees around him and even though the rain had stopped, strange low whistling howls played on the wind, ratcheting up the tension between his shoulders.

"Why did you come out here, Gerry?" he asked the darkness. "Did you come out here to—"

"—die?" Gerald spoke in his memory. "Life is so unfair, isn't it? Those poor kids probably never even knew what hit them."

Hank wished that was what had happened. But he'd watched one of them die. He'd seen with his own eyes as something sucked the life out of that boy's body, turned the skin gray and sagging, wrenched his face clean back over his skull like being sucked into an enormous vacuum. He couldn't get that image out of his head no matter what he did.

"Kids deserve to be brats for a little bit of their lives, don't they?" Gerard had continued. "I know I was. I always had to question the rules, maybe try to bend them a bit. I didn't want to believe everything was the way my parents said it was. And I got that." He'd smirked.

"I can't say I was any different," Hank had agreed, massaging his right temple. If he did this, he could almost pretend the pain wasn't as bad. He hadn't wanted to cut short his night with his friend, his one night to make sense of whatever had happened to them out on that ridge.

"I took you for a teacher's pet, Hank," Gerard had scoffed. "Aced all your classes, top marks, outdoor

63

education in college, straight into a career with the forest service?"

Hank took a pull from his beer. "I actually was failing all but one class when my dad decided to sign me up for a summer volunteering at one of the huts out here. Totally rewired my brain."

"What was the one class you weren't failing?"

"Economics."

Gerard had chuckled. "Well, you turned out alright, Ranger Feld. Though I'm sure this gig doesn't pay as well as your first trajectory may have."

"I wouldn't have graduated the next year if I hadn't gone. Would have had to stay back and take summer classes. That would have disappointed my parents a lot."

Gerard set his empty beer bottle aside and got up to retrieve another from the cooler nearby. "They must be proud of you now though?"

"They are. I think." Hank had stared at his hands as a chill rippled through him. He wasn't sure what time it was but it had gotten cold, so cold in the last ten or fifteen minutes. "We don't have much of a chance to talk actually. They live in Alaska now. They don't have great reception where they are."

"Ah," Gerard sighed as he'd settled himself back in the rocker and stared at Hank. Hank noticed there was a wistfulness in his friend's eyes, and the longer Gerard looked at him, the more Hank began to wonder if he was imagining tears in his eyes.

"Sorry," Gerard muttered, turning away. "You, um… I just…"

"Gerry?"

"This is what I had wanted to do with David a year ago. This is what we were supposed to do. And, I haven't done this with anyone since."

Hank had watched his breath puff out. "I'm sorry, Gerry."

"No, it's okay." Gerard smiled. "He would have liked you. And you'd have liked him. There's actually a lot of similarity between you, except for two things."

Hank had smiled. The cold almost hurt his face now. It was too cold for them to still be outside doing this. Despite that, he'd said, "What are they?"

"One: he never got outside his comfort zone. Ended up majoring in political science. Took a cushy job in Boston. Two: if he had to work out here in the woods all the time, he'd never have lasted. David was always afraid of the woods as a kid."

THE WOODS

11:45 A.M.

Gerard trembled in the dirt on the forest floor. He hadn't realized his fists were clutching at the strange, brittle twigs and plants on the ground. Didn't realize the hitching of his own breath as he fought back panic's razor edge. Tears stained the lines in his face.

His son was dead. David was *lost*.

Was this what awaited him at the end of his life? Was this the place he would open his eyes to, where he'd stumble around inside, shouting for help before he was dragged off to be eaten by some indefinite horrible monster? Was this where Penny would end up when she died?

Determinism closed its fingers around his fright softly. This wasn't the time to lose his mind. He had to take action now. He had to find his way out of here, back to the woods he knew, back to Hank and his friends in Cardend. He had to warn them that this was here, that it was coming for them…

But he couldn't leave David. He couldn't leave his only son like this.

Gerard gathered his wits, picked himself up out of the dirt and the blackness. He whirled around, taking shallow breaths, trying to determine which direction he'd last seen and heard the monster take David. Once he was sure, he gave pursuit.

Hiking here wasn't as easy as it was in the woods of The White Mountains National Forest. For one, there was usually a sun or moon or stars to navigate by. None of those things existed here, all plastered over by an inescapable darkness. There didn't appear to be any bodies of water either, in spite of the ground being wet and he didn't come across any as he traveled.

Other than walking in a straight line, which Gerard was fairly good at, the only other thing he could think of was to try and negotiate the forest by keeping track of landmarks. Those were almost as impossible as the other typically full-proof methods of navigation. Every tree was as tall as the one next to it. All of them were coated in moss. None differed from the others.

Gerard kept going. Every few minutes, he'd say David's name like an intonation. David had found him against all odds, as he had run around after death here. Surely, he could find his son the same way. They were *attached*. That was what David had said.

As he walked, Gerard let memories wash through his mind like the ocean lapping at a beach. Memories that were stained ochre in his mind from the summer sun. Memories that seemed to be missing bits here and there, were hazy through the middles but had definite beginnings and endings. They were out of order, no sense of time to them, but all were important.

David riding his bike without training wheels and careening down into a thorn bush by accident. Penny giving David a bath in their kitchen sink and putting his hair into a mohawk. David helping repaint the house as a summer job and knocking the paint can off the sawhorse into the grass by accident. One of their summer vacations at the camp where they cooked and ate trout while Gerard played guitar, some old Gordon Lightfoot song he used to know. One of David's baseball games. David skipping rocks in the ocean with Penny's parents, eating hot dogs by the beach, petting goats at one of the local fairs…

The memories sustained him, kept David afloat in his head.

After what felt like hours of marching through the darkness, light ebbed into Gerard's vision. A gradual orange overtook the sky between the trees and eventually they dwindled to reveal an overlook.

Knees wobbling with tire, Gerard looked out over the expanse of trees toward a monstrous structure. It shimmered with the jagged shards of what appeared to be precious stone: stone that reminded him of Shimmering Rock almost instantly. But this was much larger, several stories tall, and the stone seemed to prickle out from it all over like needles. At its base, the forest stopped in almost a perfect ring around the monolith.

Firelight flickered there in that space. And what he'd misinterpreted as bird calls at first, he now realized were the sounds of screams, their echoes tinny and far-off. The realization made nausea swim in Gerard's stomach. The lost. Those poor people were down there and something terrible was happening to them. Inside of that nausea, he knew David was down there with them.

Gerard started down the hill toward the structure. What was he going to do? How was he going to get David out of there without alerting those monsters? He didn't have a plan and as he scrambled to come up with one, he kept going in spite of not having one.

He'd already lost David once. He couldn't lose him again.

THE WOODS

10:50 P.M.

Hank was lost. The trail wasn't in front of or behind him anymore, the land veiled in almost absolute darkness. Hank had promised Andy he wouldn't do this. He'd said he would keep his wits about him and would make sure not to end up in a way where he'd need to be rescued, too.

The headlamp light flickered and Hank instinctively unzipped his waist belt pocket, fishing around for the extra batteries he kept there.

When he didn't find any, he grimaced. He had forgotten to put new ones in after his last excursion.

Racked with new guilt and self-loathing, he unbuckled his pack and slung it off his shoulders, then knelt down to rifle through it for his extra headlamp.

He was coming apart at the seams. The headache was excruciating now. He had always been methodical about the job before this. He had prepared for every eventuality when he geared up and went into the wilderness because he never knew what he'd come across. He had to be prepared because *he* was supposed to save *them*: the lost, the inexperienced.

Except for today. Today, he'd let panic get the better of him. Today, he'd thrown himself into the woods like an idiot in search of his friend and was no better than other unprepared hikers who got in over their heads.

Exchanging the faltering headlamp for a new one, Hank clicked it on in time to see a figure stumble out of the darkness ahead of him. All the hairs on his arms stood.

"Gerard!" he yelled.

The figure turned in his direction. "Is someone out there?"

Not Gerard. It was a woman's voice.

Hank recalled Dan's message on the radio. Could this have been the hiker's friend, the one that was supposed to have gone back to the car for help?

"Hey!" he called again, zipping up his pack and securing it once more. "Stay right there. I'll come to you!"

"I've been out here for hours," the woman whimpered. "I heard someone else calling out though. I was trying to find them and then…"

"Hang on," Hank said, edging over the dark landscape until he came to the woman. She was in her late twenties, maybe early thirties. Long dark hair was pulled back into a ponytail beneath her winter beanie. She'd taken off her puffy jacket and tied it around her torso, pushed up the sleeves on her shirt to her elbows.

He had thought the temperature change might have been self-induced at first, another side-effect of the headache, or the realization that he was sicker than he'd previously imagined. Now, he knew it wasn't just him. It was this place, this wild space within the woods that seemed to have no end.

"What's your name?" Hank asked her, removing his pack once more. He pulled his Nalgene out and handed it to her.

Unscrewing the cap, she greedily took a few gulps before replying, "Andrea."

"Andrea, you said you heard someone in here?"

Another few gulps. "Yeah, thanks." She handed it back. "Yeah. Like, someone else couldn't find their way out of here. I mean, it's so fucking pitch black. I didn't think it would get this dark in here?"

"There's a lot of cloud cover. That limits the light." Hank realized that there hadn't been any rain since he'd entered the darker part of the woods. It hadn't seemed like it was going to let up any time soon, either.

"I don't know where that guy went," she said. "I was just trying to get back to the car. My friend fell and twisted her ankle on the trail. I was going to see if I could get a signal so I could call the ranger station but there's been no reception."

Hank took a chug from the water bottle before sliding it back into his bag. "Guess it's a good thing we ended up out here, huh?"

"Did you find Harriet?"

"My colleagues did. Last I heard, they were taking her back to the lot and they'd called for medical to meet them there."

Andrea exhaled and a small smile tugged at her mouth. "Thank God."

Hank pulled his GPS from his jacket pocket. It's tiny screen created a halo of eerie light around his fingers as he checked the map. Strange. It showed him in the middle of nowhere. No distinguishing landmarks, no trails ahead of or behind him. When he tried to widen the map to see a larger area, it remained featureless.

"That's really weird," he muttered.

"What's wrong?" Andrea's voice had an edge to it.

"Nothing," he was quick to say. "We're going to head back in the direction I just came from, okay?"

"But what about that other guy? There's someone else out here, isn't there? And you were looking for them?"

Hank nodded. "You saw him?"

"Not clearly. But I know he's in here somewhere. You can't just leave him, can you?"

Hank's gut turned. "Normally, I'd send a signal via GPS for the team to come and find us. I'm getting interference though. We'll have to hike out until we can get a clear signal. And I don't have enough supplies for the both of us to last out here the whole night."

She frowned. "What if no one can get out here to help you look?"

"Are you okay to walk, Andrea?"

"Yeah, I'm fine, but—"

"We really should go."

Every word he said felt like a needle digging into his skin. He didn't want to leave Gerard out here. But it wasn't up to him now. The GPS not working made him flashback to being in the woods weeks ago, to being near Shimmering Rock and having his GPS declare it had no signal. They couldn't stay.

"Who is he?" she said as she took a few steps toward him. "The other lost guy?"

"His name is Gerard Castle. He's in his seventies." Hank wasn't sure why that was the defining sentence he chose. He could have said "he's my friend". He could have said "he has a wife at home". He could have said "he's an experienced hiker". But he chose fragility. He chose the thing he was most afraid of being Gerard's downfall out here. And it pushed the needle further.

She stopped. "Oh my God. We can't just leave him?" Quieter. "Can we?"

We can't. Hank's throat tightened with every step he took away from the woods.

"I hate this," Andrea said, a tremor in her voice. She was cold. He reached into the hip belt pocket and produced a hand-warmer which he tossed to her. "Tear the plastic and give that a shake. It'll help."

She did as she was hold and Hank heard a sigh of relief from behind him.

They walked in silence for the next few minutes. Hank hoped they were heading in the right direction. He had no way of knowing, no way of figuring out where he was in here. The trail had been long disused, long abandoned. All the trail markers had worn away and new vegetation had sprouted over the path people used to walk. All he had to do was keep going until he had a signal though. All he had to do was keep them both alive and awake until morning.

"I'm sorry," Andrea said suddenly.

He looked over his shoulder at her. "Why?"

"If I hadn't gotten lost, you could still be looking for that guy. What was his name? Gerald?"

"Gerard. He'd kill me if he heard me calling him that though." He smirked. "He prefers Gerry."

"You know him?"

"Yeah. He's a friend."

Andrea stared at her boots. "Fuck."

Hank turned around and continued.

We can't. We can't. We can—

A screech broke Hank's mantra followed by the feeling of a hand trying to grab his before being snatched away.

Hank spun in time to see Andrea being yanked back into the blackness, a yelp ejecting out of her mouth before being drowned in silence. Leaves rustled and crunched as something ran into the thicket.

"Andrea!" he yelled. Panting, Hank swiveled his head, the light from his headlamp barely cutting through the darkness. A new trail scraped through the leaves on the forest floor, along with broken saplings and ferns.

Far off, he heard her scream.

"Andrea!" Hank blindly threw himself into the bushes after her.

THE WOODS

2:30 P.M.

Gerard crossed the dark landscape, threading himself between the mossy trees. He had trouble taking his eyes off the sky. It was a color that reminded him of a forest fire, of danger surging nearby. An oppressive smog with the flicker of flames roiling behind it.

Rational people wouldn't be trying to go deeper into a place like this. They would have turned around long ago, and he should have, too. His brain sent up signal flares that what he was doing was insane. His chest led him, his heart tethered to David, to the son he'd lost too early. If his soul was the only thing left of him to save, Gerard had to try. He wouldn't be able to live with himself if he didn't.

But the closer he came to the screams and shouts, the more he felt terror bloom within him. Finally, he found himself at the edge of the woods looking out over a stone dais, pillars of shining rock, and the Lost themselves.

There were four men and women with their wrists bound behind each stone column. Torches burned in between them, casting wobbly light and shadows over each soul. One was just a girl, barely twelve, maybe thirteen. She sobbed and called for her mother and each time she did made Gerard's throat burn.

Another man in his forties or fifties was shouting threats into the air, each one charged with mania. "You'd better let me the fuck out of here! Let me go!"

Gerard recognized the voice. It was the person he'd tried to help in the forest. The guy was bloodied, his left shoulder mangled. Gerard could see the flesh dangling from it in places.

David was at the pillar to the man's left. Gerard's heart soared. His son was unconscious, his jacket torn and his t-shirt spotted with gobs of red.

He had to get to him. He had to get him free.

Fear pinned Gerard in place. Not yet. Something wasn't right here…

The last of the Lost was an older Black woman who stared over her shoulder into the mouth of a darkening cavern in the face of the Monolith. Even from where he stood, Gerard could hear her panicked recitation of the Lord's Prayer.

Why were they here? Who had tied them up?

Gerard found his gaze glued to the darkness of the hole in the Monolith. What was in there? He could swear he caught a hint of movement in the gloom but couldn't make it into a definitive shape in his mind.

As the thought of the wolves crept into his head, a

baying rumbled from the grass ahead of him, just over a small crest on the other side of the stone dais.

The thing the sound belonged to materialized out of the darkness, form shaped from murkiness. The creature was far uglier than anything Gerard had seen. A powerful body that could have stood level with his shoulders marched forward between the shining pillars. The snout was canid, though its movements were quick and jerky, almost like a lizard. Its mouth revealed thousands of pin-like fangs that gleamed against the firelight around them. It whipped its head toward the sky and let out a piercing call.

Gerard pressed his hands against his ears trying to block out the harshness of the shrill sound. This thing had killed those kids on the ridge at Shimmering Rock. This thing had stolen his son and brought him here. But it hadn't killed him. What was all this—

Another howl caught him off guard and Gerard crouched instinctively as another beast emerged from the surrounding shadows, its talons clicking against the stone as it joined the other one.

They raised their muzzles to the sky, their eyes reflecting a cold glow. They let out a collective howl, more like a groan: a sound steeped in wretchedness; in emptiness.

David woke up.

Gerard's breath hitched.

"Oh God!" the other man cried. "Oh, fuck!"

The girl screamed and squeezed her eyes shut.

In the resounding echo of the creature's call was a strange static that filled the air, white noise that made

Gerard want to clear his ears. It was the kind of congestion he'd felt with a cold, like his head was full of water and other sounds could barely be heard around it. Even the terrified sounds of the Lost were muffled by its presence.

Inside of the static, something pitched. A sound like coarse sand raised and lowered and flowed behind it. Like…talking through the static on a radio?

Inside the cavern, the darkness moved.

The static became a voice, a voice that was almost a whisper though it resonated through Gerard's head, humming, making his jaw lock in fear.

Lost…

The girl shrieked.

The man beside David let out a strange laugh cry that reminded Gerard of a sheep. "Wh-what is that?" he sputtered.

All lost…

David pulled against his restraints; his eyes locked on the girl. "It's okay," he yelled to her. "You're going to be okay. If I can just…"

The old woman had slumped down to her knees and whispered her prayers all the faster.

Forgotten, the voice continued and Gerard felt his eyes watering at the strange pressure it caused in his head whenever it spoke. *Flattened.*

Gerard frowned. What did that mean? He noticed a figure at the edge of the shadows in the cave, its foot the only definite thing he could make out. But as it emerged and each facet was lit by the waxing flames of the nearby torches, Gerard's breath vanished and his entire body broke into an icy sweat.

Two legs appeared, coated in a crusted yellow skin that glistened against the firelight. Their steps were slow, as if the thing using them hadn't walked in a long time. As its torso emerged, Gerard saw that it, too, was covered in the same skin, blistered in puss-filled wounds, wrinkled and mottled brown in places. It was holding something in its hands, which draped down toward the cavern floor. They scratched against the rock with each swing of its step.

Porous, it said. *Soured.*

The shadows slid back to reveal two broad, sinewy arms with large hands. *Not holding something,* Gerard realized. The claws that dangled from it were razor-sharp and reached the floor just barely.

Ragged.

The face. Gerard's stomach turned. His arms gave out. The world spun as he lay on his side, staring at its face.

It had no eyes; its nose two pinpricks in the place above a mouth without lips. Coated in mottled yellow like aged glue, the head crested into a giant curled horn that twisted on itself. As it turned, Gerard saw it was hollow, its end like a cornucopia, segmented…woven, the same texture as the rest of its body.

Now the other man was screaming.

David's face was twisted in revulsion. He cried.

Gerard's mouth tasted like acid, like the tang of copper and the bile that was caught in his throat.

Stained, the voice spoke, the desire in its tone sickening. *Rooted inside.*

It staggered to the pillar closest to it: the man next to David.

"Holy shit! Holy Christ!" the man squealed, fumbling to get himself as far away from the thing as possible.

David did the same, leaning hard.

The old woman was crying now. Her sobs mixed with the girl's.

Corrupt fire within, it buzzed. Its hand snapped out.

Gerard lost control and puked.

When he looked up again, two long talons had skewered the man's neck while the other three pierced his jaw, through his ear canal, and the skin at the top of his head.

The man should have been dead.

But he thrashed. He screamed. He wailed.

The creature slashed through the bonds holding the man to the stone and raised his body into the air to bring him up to its face, to the horn.

Gerard gagged, wiping the saliva from his lips. He couldn't tear his eyes away.

Acid thrones floating.

The last word came out as a hoarse whisper.

The man whimpered.

Suddenly, two holes opened on the creature's face. As Gerard beheld their bright red cat-like stare, he realized he had been wrong. It had eyes all along.

The smell of ozone hit Gerard as the torches flickered and darkness shrouded the dais. Everything went black.

His senses drowned; Gerard only had a moment to panic before the fires roared back to life.

The horn had engulfed the man's head, both clawed hands now spearing the quivering body in place as the thing ate. Viscous, dark tendrils flowed down the man's neck to his seizing chest.

The wolves snarled from their places around the dais. Their tails danced, as if reveling in the torture.

They were distracted. This was the perfect time for him to sneak in. But Gerard couldn't make himself, horror gluing him to the ground just as it had in the forest.

Yanking him free of the horn, the monster flung the mangled man across the dais. He tumbled in a heap at the wolves feet.

To.

The.

Center.

Gerard blinked. That had been the first coherent thing it had said.

One of the four-legged creatures sank its teeth into the man's torso before lifting him off the ground and bounding into the reeds a few feet from Gerard's right.

A chorus of cries made Gerard focus back on the monstrous thing before him. He had to figure out how to distract it so he could cut David free. He glanced down at his waist pack. The pepper spray.

Pure, the voice purred as it focused on the screaming girl.

Gerard readied himself to open his mouth, to shout.

"Me!"

He hadn't said a thing.

"Take me instead!" David yelled.

Gerard's skin prickled.

The creature spun back toward him. It crossed the distance to David in no time, one of its claws tearing through the restraints while the other one slammed into David's shoulder. He choked on a scream.

Picking himself up, Gerard ran from his cover into the clearing. As his fingers curled around the nearest torch, he felt warm breath on his back seconds before something slammed into him.

Gerard crashed to the ground, pain igniting in his chest immediately. He moaned. It hurt to breathe. Each time he tried to inhale, something stabbed him.

"DAD!" David yelled.

Gerard flipped his face to see his son, to see the thing holding him there. Its face was turned toward him now, the red eyes closed, the gaping cornucopia horn like an endless gullet.

He tried to put an arm under him to help him get up, but something pushed him down. A snout entered Gerard's vision, opening to show a black tongue and nacreous fangs.

Living. The creature holding David cocked its head.

Gerard tried to muster up the courage to say something but his lungs screamed and he couldn't seem to get any air into them.

The creature ripped its claws from David and stomped across the dais to the wolf and Gerard.

How?

Gerard wheezed as air finally rushed down into his system. Tears raced down his cheeks as he took short, desperate breaths against the pressure weighing him down.

The sharp end of a long claw scraped at his chin.

You do not belong yet.

Gerard stared into the horn. Eyes blinked deep inside: red and watching.

In one fluent motion, the horned monster slashed its claws at the wolf holding Gerard down, impaling its torso as it shrieked. Gerard curled into himself, watching as shadows like blood slithered from the open wounds on the nightmarish creature.

Open walls to the living earth. Insipid beasts. Left open.

Gerard slid his hand into his waist belt and grabbed the pepper spray. His eyes fell to David's form, which lay on the stone dais, holding his shoulder. No blood seeped from his new wound, but the skin and muscle were shredded.

Letting the wolf slide off of its claws, the horned monster moved back to Gerard's side. *Must make this correct. Balance. Reset the walls.*

Biting his lip, Gerard rolled away, every movement sending spears through in his chest. As soon as he was clear, he lifted the pepper spray canister and thumbed down the release button.

The stream splattered against the monster's horn, and its face. With a primal squeal, it fell, claws buried in the ground.

Gerard pushed himself, every breath burning. Climbing to his feet, he limped across the stone dais towards David, falling to his knees in front of him.

"Davey."

David looked up into his eyes, shock widening them. "You shouldn't have followed. Dad. You shouldn't…"

"I couldn't leave you." Gerard started to reach for him but remembered the cold and how it burned. He retracted his hand. "You need to get up. Get out of here. Now."

"No, Dad, you're hurt. I can't—"

The wail ripped through Gerard's head, a sound that made him clap his hands over his ears again, made him want to bury his head underground.

"Please. If this is the last time I see you," Gerard answered before taking in David's face once more. "Don't end like *this*. Not like *this*."

David got up, his injured shoulder hanging like dead weight at his side. "I love you."

"Love you, too," Gerard choked out.

Gerard turned away, turned toward the trapped women on the other side of the dais who were shouting and crying and bucking for an escape. Collecting one of the torches, he hobbled to the old woman's pillar and held the fire to her bonds. Within moments, they crackled and fell apart. Not even waiting, Gerard moved to the girl.

"It's okay, sweetie," he said, watching the flames eat the vines holding her there. "You'll be out of here soon."

They snapped.

Gerard swung around, searching for where he'd entered the fray. Something caught him and twisted and the feeling of popping in his chest forced all the breath from his lungs. He looked down to see the thin, sallow claws with their black tips sinking deeper into his abdomen. Blood trickled down his light blue shirt.

Blinking, he lifted his gaze to the horn-headed creature, its eyes open on its face, like shining red car taillights, blaring into him.

Corrupted, it seethed.

Then, with a casual flick, it tossed him away. Gerard's body pummeled into the ground like a sack of meat, as his spirit barreled past it into the bowels of the earth. Darkness enshrouded him.

THE WOODS

11:30 P.M.

Hank wasn't sure how long he'd been running. He was barely aware of his surroundings anymore. His head throbbed like someone was beating on it. His legs felt dead and exhausted and the pack only seemed to grow heavier and heavier with each step he made.

Was Andrea still alive? Was Gerard? Was *he* still?

Hank didn't remember collapsing, only that the feeling of the cool plants under him felt good, their leaves caressing his face. He felt like he could melt into them. All he wanted to do was sleep.

In the back of his brain, he heard Evie calling his name. As Hank's eyes closed, he thought he saw a shape move in the bushes before him.

THE WOODS

10:00 P.M.

Gerard dreamed of tree tops enshrouded in velvety darkness that called to him, asked to wrap around him like a warm quilt. There was a smell of evergreen, of rich earth, of autumn, of moss... They were smells that comforted him, pulled him back to a time in his youth where the mysteries of the woods were invigorating, new, and prickled with dangerous potential. He let himself fall into that memory; into them.

And when he came to, the quilt was yanked away.

He didn't remember opening his eyes, only that the tree tops became tree trunks and he was surrounded by them. Gerard shivered and instinctively grabbed at his abdomen as the memories crashed back on him like a wave.

Stabbed. He'd been stabbed. Brutally. Horribly. But there was nothing. His body was whole.

As his sights adjusted to the blue darkness, he

recognized the curl of smoke as it rose from expired torches across from him. Shapes grew clearer. Pillars of stone. The dais beneath his feet. And the bodies strewn all around him.

Gerard stumbled to the body of the old woman; her head was shielded in a cloud of smoky darkness. He couldn't see her eyes. But inky sludge pooled beneath her. "No…" he uttered as he looked to his left and saw the girl's body, her legs tangled in ferns at the edge of the dais. Her head was similarly shielded. Another body lay nearby, this one completely covered in the swirling blackness.

How had this happened? He'd saved them. He'd cut them free. He'd—

Gerard's gaze settled on the last body crumpled at the mouth of the cave, the body wearing a familiar leather jacket and tarnished jeans.

A noise like an off-key violin escaped his throat as he scrambled over to it. "David? David?"

What remained of David's face was enfolded by the darkness, the dirt shifted in frantic scrapes where a struggle had occurred. The oily fluid coating his Guns n' Roses shirt glimmered, even with no light. Gerard forgot about the burning cold, a sorrow rising in his body with ferocity like the sun as he reached out and tried to cradle his son's body.

He touched it. He touched the smooth wrinkles of the leather jacket, the muscles of David's bicep before yanking his hand back in panic. It only took him a second to reach back in, to envelop David and pull his body into his arms fully. Gerard choked on his tears and memories of his son as time stood still.

THE WOODS

MIDNIGHT

Hank shivered against the base of the tree trunk. He had failed. He'd failed Gerard. He'd failed Andrea. He'd failed his boss and co-workers. He'd failed Evie. And now he was going to die out here in these woods because he'd been too eager to prove that he was ready to be out here.

Struggling to unzip the pocket in his waist belt, Hank pulled out his phone. Though the battery was nearly dead, he still thumbed through his recent calls to find Gerard's phone number and dialed it. The crackle of static reverberated emptily through his head as he put the phone to his ear and waited. No ringing. Gerard's bright voice answered with the usual voicemail request.

It beeped.

"Gerry," Hank said, trying to keep his teeth from chattering. "Wherever you are, if you hear this, I wanted to say how sorry I am. I tried to find you. I tried to bring

you back. I couldn't."
    At the other end of the static, a voice responded.

THE WOODS

MIDNIGHT

Wind fluttered against Gerard as he lifted his head. He wasn't sure how long he'd been there on his knees in the dirt embracing David. But something called to him on that breeze, like a whisper, like something he'd heard in a dream. Something different than the deadening sadness that coursed through him. A flicker, like a matchlight in the blackness of familiarity. Of home.

Gerard forced himself to let go of David and stood, no longer feeling the tiredness of his old bones, the exhaustion of his muscles. The energy gave him pause. His body hadn't felt this way in years. Even when he'd done yoga to keep limber and hiked for cardio, old age had weakened him. But this… he didn't feel like he was in his mid-seventies. The strength was like that of his thirties.

"Gerry…"

His name. Someone was speaking his name and it

was carrying on the wind like dandelion seeds.

He knew that voice. Didn't he?

He did. Hank. That was Hank.

Gerard's shoulders stiffened. If Hank was out here looking for him in these woods, he was in danger.

Crossing the rest of the dais to the edge of the woods, Gerard cast a glance back at the remains strewn about the altar, at the smudge of David's body as the darkness from the cave seemed to grow to envelop it.

He couldn't save David. But he could still save Hank. His friend. The man who reminded him of who David could have become.

Hank, who still had a daughter to take care of. Who still had the ability to do great things with the rest of his life.

Gerard ran through the woods, dipping over the uneven landscape, following the echo of Hank's voice on the back of each gust.

"I'm coming," he chanted to himself. "I'm coming."

The trees morphed around him, their trunks widening in breadth, the foliage expanding, the orange fire sky vanishing into nothingness.

Hank lay before him, curled up against the base of a tree as he murmured into his phone. He was practically white, sweating profusely, his clothes soaked.

"Hank!" Gerard crouched next to him and touched his hand.

Hank snapped out of his stupor, crying out. He wildly looked around.

He looked *through* Gerard.

The realization was soft. It struck Gerard like being tickled with a feather. His fingers had gone through Hank. Hank couldn't see him.

Gerard's throat closed up. Panic slathered him like paint as he fell onto his butt. It made sense. It all made sense. The other body he couldn't make out in the darkness at the dais had been...

"Gerry?" Hank said into the phone. "Was that your voice?"

Hank couldn't see him. But he had *heard* him.

"Buddy, I'm here," he said, playing along. "Where are you?"

Hank's face straightened, his brows furrowing. "Where am I? Where are you? I'm out here looking for you. You marked a map. I came to find you."

The map. Gerard instantly hated himself for leaving it. His thoughts returned to David and he felt himself go under for a moment, the grief too much to bear.

"Hello?" Hank called, panting heavily. "Damn phone. Come on!"

"I'm still here, champ," Gerard said. "I'm at the trailhead. I want you to come meet me."

Hank's mouth soured. "You're in the trail head parking lot? How?"

"Don't ask questions, Hank. I need you to get out of the woods and come find me."

"But..." Hank swallowed. "I'm just so tired right now."

"Get up, Hank."

With a grunt, Hank pushed himself up from a sitting position and stood. As he swung his pack up onto his back, he spoke again, "What did you mean by your message? That you saw David's ghost?"

"I was tired, Hank," Gerard lied, feeling the claws of sadness hook him once more. "I never went into the woods. I went to Middlehitch for the day. Just got back."

"Middlehitch," Hank muttered as he started walking. "Yeah."

Hank trudged through the woods, Gerard following behind.

"There was another woman out here," Hank said. "She was lost. Andrea. Something got her. I think maybe it was the same thing we saw at Shimmering Rock…"

Gerard closed his eyes. Behind the closed lids, he felt an erratic pulsing, followed by a glowing pinkish hue like a flashlight being shone through someone's hand, highlighting the skin, the blood…

"Do me a favor, champ," Gerard said, cutting him off. "Dan's got you on his GPS. He's tracking you. You need to head southwest, okay?"

"How does Dan have me on his GPS? Mine can't even get a signal in here?"

"We've got you, okay? Go southwest. That's the way out."

Hank shifted slightly to his right and kept on.

The pulsing throbbed in Gerard's temples the closer they grew. *A heartbeat,* he realized. A glow became visible in the unending darkness, like a soft lamp.

Hank's footsteps, which had started out strong, were growing smaller, turning into a shamble. "I'm just so tired," he whispered into the phone.

Gerard turned to him. "What was that song? From

last night at the bar?" He snapped his fingers. "Carry On My Wayward Son. Let's sing it. You and me. Let's go."

After an uncomfortable grunt from Hank, he awkwardly sang the first line, followed up by Gerard with the second. They made their way toward the glow, trading off with each line from the song.

Half way through the second verse, Hank collapsed.

"Hank!" Gerard shouted. "Hank!"

He mumbled incoherently but didn't get up.

"Damn it." Gerard could barely think with the pounding in his head, now as striking as ever. They were so close to that glow, to finding Andrea.

As Gerard walked over to her, he stopped cold. She was breathing shallowly. Her hand was pressed against her ribs as she lay strewn in the weeds; her hair tossed over her face. A knife was clutched in her other hand. Andrea had fought back enough to get free from whatever monster had tried to take her.

The throbbing in his head was like cannon fire. Inexplicably, he found himself getting closer and closer to her, as though her body exuded a nostalgia, a smell like his mother's chocolate chip cookies in the oven, a sound like birdsong and his wife's beautiful timbre, a feeling of afternoon sunlight and an iced tea tanging on his tongue…

He fell through the ground, fell into a tide of blackness that faded into those treetops he'd seen not so long ago. Andrea floated there, her eyes wide, hands reaching for his. He reached back too late and watched as her body plummeted down into the trees while he soared back up, back toward the waiting ground, back toward Andrea's body.

THE WOODS

12:25 A.M.

A light shone behind Hank's closed lids. He winced as he cracked them open, as he exhaled. "What?"

"You're okay," a woman's voice said, putting a supportive hand under his armpit. "One, two, three…UP!"

Hank sat up with her help, letting his vision come back. "Andrea, I thought you were dead."

She swallowed and nodded. "Me, too. Good thing I found you. You were pretty out of it."

Hank took a deep breath. "I got through to Gerard. He's back at the parking lot. Apparently he never came out here."

Andrea grabbed his hand and pulled him to his feet, before seething and holding her ribs.

"That looks bad," Hank said. "Are you okay to walk?"

"I'll be fine," she said confidently. "We need to go. Before you go out like a light again."

"Again?"

She cocked her head. "Well, I assume you didn't choose to fall asleep here, right?"

Hank gave her that one. "Before I 'went out', Gerard had said to go south west. That's were we probably should head."

"I talked to him before your phone died," she blurted quickly. "He said we needed to head south now. Just straight south. That should take us to the trail."

"My phone died?" Confused, Hank searched for it on the forest floor in vain.

"I've got it. In my bag," Andrea said. "Let's go."

The hike was slow going. Hank's body hurt everywhere. His skin sizzled and was slick with sweat, his feet hurt and his back ached from hauling his pack around all night. But Andrea forged ahead, in spite of her injury and he was inspired to keep going after her.

A pale light cast a stream through the demented trees toward them, followed by a rushing sound that felt familiar and instantly made Hank want to tear up with happiness. Rain. The beautiful sound of rain.

"Come on!" Andrea grabbed his hand and pulled him along until they erupted out of the filmy darkness and into the blue night.

Cold drops splashed down across Hank's face, chest, and arms. He let a few drops run past his lips, down his throat. He hadn't thought he'd ever miss this feeling; didn't think he'd wonder if he'd ever experience it again.

Hank let a small laugh escape before looking over at Andrea. "We made it."

"We've almost made it, champ," she said. "We still

have to get to the parking lot."

They donned their coats again, shielding themselves from the downpour and picked along the slippery path, their boots splashing in the mud. Only a few yards away from the dark edge of the woods, the rain turned to sleet and then to snow.

Hank tucked his hands into the front pockets of his jacket, having taken his gloves off somewhere in the forest. He stared at Andrea's back, a niggling feeling crawling its way up through his brain. "You called me 'champ' back there."

She hesitated mid-step.

"It's funny. Gerard used to do that. Did your dad ever call you that?"

Andrea glanced back at him. "Y-yeah. He always wanted a boy."

Hank's radio let out a garbled blend of static before Dan's voice echoed over it. "Cooper to Feld. God damn it, Hank. Where the hell are you?"

Hank picked the radio from his belt and said, "I'm here."

"Jesus H. Christ! Where the hell have you been? I called in almost the entire Pemigewasset S&R to search for you."

"We're on the Wingbeat Trail. I've got that partner to the missing hiker you've found, Andrea, with me," he answered. "A little banged up. She'll need medical attention."

"What about Gerard?" Dan asked. "Did you ever find Gerard?"

Hank froze. "What do you mean? He's not out at the

trail head?"

"No, Hank. He's not here."

"But…" Hank struggled to recall his conversation on the phone. "I called him. He said he was out there."

"You called him? Hank, I've been trying to call you for the last three hours. I haven't been able to get through. Even if he was here with us, he wouldn't have been able to get through to you."

Hank let out a breath through his nose. "But, Andrea said she—"

She was gone.

Hank spun around, searching the trail for her. "Andrea?" He took a few steps further. "Andrea?"

She didn't respond.

"Hank?" Dan called from the radio.

"I just lost her. I swear she was right here a moment ago."

"Stay where you are, Hank. Andy and a few others are on their way to you."

It didn't make any sense. She'd been there. He'd heard and seen her as clear as day. She'd pulled him along until they'd gotten out of the darkness. She couldn't have just vanished…

Hank leaned against the base of a cedar tree to shelter from the snow and stared down at his feet. How much of that had he dreamed? How much had been real?

Moments later, Andy's headlamp pierced the darkness. "There you are, you lying motherfucker," he greeted trudging toward Hank. "I told you it was a bad idea. Dan nearly took my head off for leaving you out here."

Hank's stomach twisted. "Gerry is still out there, Andy."

Andy squatted a little to look at Hank's face. "You do not look good. Do we need to cart you out of here on a stretcher or are you going to walk out on your own?"

Hank bit his lip to keep back the tears. "I'll walk. I'm good."

Andy set his hand on Hank's shoulder. "Come on. Let's get you home, huh?"

12:40 A.M.

Red and blue lights welcomed Hank to the parking lot at the head of the Hatchling Spring Trail. As much as Hank wanted to go straight home, Andy steered him toward the nearest ambulance where Dan awaited with a disapproving frown.

"This could have been really bad, Hank," he said as the paramedics wrapped a mylar blanket around Hank's shoulders and told him to sit on a stretcher.

They shined lights in his eyes. Asked him to recite his name. The year. His birthday. What town he lived in. He answered each one never taking his eyes off the forest.

"Hank?"

He let his gaze drift back to Dan. "They want to take you to Cardend Memorial for observation. Do you want me to call Melissa?"

Hank shook his head. "No."

He laid back on the stretcher and they strapped him

down. Dan climbed into the bus and took a seat next to him before the paramedics closed the doors.

"I heard him, Dan. I could swear I heard him."

"That's what happens with hallucinations. They feel real. You'd stake your life on them."

"What about Andrea?" Hank said. "She's still out there."

"We'll keep a party out looking for her. But in this cold?" Dan shrugged.

The ambulance gave a trill as it rumbled over the dirt lot and slowly pulled out onto the road. Somewhere between there and the hospital, Hank fell asleep to the sound of the heart monitor's steady beep.

THE NOTCH ROAD

12:50 A.M.

Gerard stared up at his car from the bottom of the ditch, his breath raggedly cutting from his throat. He was freezing and his ribs killed. He stared down at Andrea's hands, at her thin delicate skin, at her nails.

What had he done?

Cautiously climbing up the rocks that lined the roadside, Gerard approached his car. Half way up the hill, he heard something and turned to study the woods behind him.

They were dark, cascaded by snow. He couldn't see anything in them.

Boots slipping and sliding, Gerard got to the car and tried the handle. Locked.

He didn't have his keys. His keys were on his body lying in the middle of that stone dais in the woods. He could never go back there. He *would* never go back there.

Gerard glanced up the road. His cabin was only a

mile or two north of there. He knew it was still unlocked and if not, there was at least a spare key he could get in with. He wouldn't be able to stay there, but he'd have time to figure out what to do next.

Something shrieked in the trees.

Gerard turned as a black shape hurled itself over the lip of the embankment and slammed into him. Andrea's body snapped against the frame of the car like a twig and in a second, Gerard felt the Woods' call, the suspension in the air as he hovered over them before opening his eyes to the smooth snow-layered pavement.

As he lay there, he listened to the tearing of flesh as the wolf feasted on Andrea's body and the shrill screech of metal on metal as the car was torn to shreds in its frenzy.

RANGER STATION

7:30 A.M.

Hank walked through the doors of his work and emptiness walked with him.

Maggie looked up from staring at the computer screen at her desk and her eyes rounded. "What are you doing here?" She got to her feet and walked to him. "I thought you were supposed to be getting some rest, Hank?"

"They've got me on about three different kinds of pills from generic painkillers to migraine medicine. Besides, I can't sleep."

She touched his arm sympathetically. "Can I get you some coffee?"

"Absolutely."

She walked into the kitchen as Dan appeared from his office. "You're not supposed to be driving. Are you trying to put yourself into an early grave?" his boss asked.

"I need to be useful. Melissa has Evie until this afternoon. I can't just sit around at home and watch television like everything is okay." Hank frowned. "Please."

Dan's eyes darkened. "We found Gerard's car early this morning."

Hank's hopes plummeted. "Where?"

"On the Notch road. In the same spot where his son was found."

He *had* dreamed it, Hank realized, his hopes sinking. That entire conversation with Gerard that he thought he'd had on the phone was all in his head.

"It was torn to pieces. And there was blood."

Hank's mouth cracked. "Wh—What?"

"It looks like a bear might have…" Dan let the rest of the sentence hang.

Hank shook his head. "He could still be out there: injured."

"The amount of blood around that car…"

"But no body, right? Until its tested, Dan, we have to keep looking," Hank said, his gaze fierce.

Dan flashed him a pitiful look.

Maggie returned with Hank's mug of coffee. "I made some fliers. I figured it's not a bad idea to put them around town. Or maybe go out and ask some of those Airbnb camp people if they've seen anything. They're pretty close to that spot in the woods where you were hiking at last night."

Dan seemed eager to be done with the conversation. He nodded. "Take a stack of them and drive out there. See if anyone has anything to say."

"Yeah. It's worth a shot."

8:00 A.M.

A half an hour later, Hank steered his Jeep down a winding dirt drive toward the first cabin on his list. While it was rare for anyone to be renting out here this late in the season, Andy knew for a fact that this camp was occupied because he'd asked the owner, who he was fishing buddies with, about a lone woman he'd seen in town a couple times.

He was probably asking to see if he could get a date, Hank frowned.

A small cabin emerged from the trees in the early morning sunlight. A woman with long red hair stood on the front porch, wiping at her pants frantically. As he parked, he spied her picking up her coffee mug and watching him quizzically.

Hank opened his car door, his shadow lean and long against the pine needles and dirt. Leaning back into fetch the stack of fliers from the passenger seat, he realized with a groan that Maggie had misspelled Gerard's name on the flier as "Gerald". He shut the door and rounded the car.

The woman on the porch seemed alarmed. She seemed like she didn't want him here at all.

Hank pushed the discomfort down with the rest of his ailments and pressed on, climbing the porch steps until he stood facing her. "Good morning, ma'am."

DEDICATION

This story was for my friend, Paul McGurren, who passed away earlier on this year to cancer. He was one of the kindest, funniest, and best storytellers I have ever known.

PHOTO BY COLIN BOROWSKE ©2021

Katherine Silva is a Maine horror author, a connoisseur of coffee, and victim of cat shenanigans. She is a two-time Maine Literary Award finalist for speculative fiction and a member of the Horror Writers of Maine, The Horror Writers Association, and New England Horror Writers Association. Katherine is also editor-in-chief of Strange Wilds Press and Dark Taiga Creative Writing Consultations. A sequel to *THE WILD DARK* entitled, *THE WILD FALL*, is now available. *LOST OBLIVION* is the latest release in The Wild Oblivion series, a direct sequel to *HALLOWED OBLIVION*.